MW00465860

HEALING HOPE

PJ FIALA

COPYRIGHT

Printed in the United States of America

First published 2022

Fiala, PJ

HEALING HOPE / PJ Fiala

p. cm.

1. Romance—Fiction. 2. Romance—Suspense. 3. Romance
- Military

I. Title – HEALING HOPE

Paperback ISBN-13: 978-1-942618-88-1

DEDICATION

I've had so many wonderful people come into my life and I want you all to know how much I appreciate it. From each and every reader who takes the time out of their days to read my stories and leave reviews, thank you.

My beautiful, smart and fun Road Queens, who play games with me, post fun memes, keep the conversation rolling and help me create these captivating characters, places, businesses and more. Thank you ladies for your ideas, support and love. The following characters and places were created by:

Creed Rowan - Barb Keller

Hope Dumond - Kim Ruiz and Nicky Ortiz

Kole Dumond - Marilyn Oshnock Powell

Carolyne Dumond - Julia Murphy

Mitch Dumond - Arlene Miklovic

Darcy Jo Peters - Donna Perry Byrd

Wesley Watts - Karen Cranford LeBeau

Doctor Alex Stafford - Lyne Carroll

Byte Me - LeighAnn Fender

Rose Gardens Mortuary - Mary Lou Melzer

Shayla Jones - Kristi Hombs Kopydlowski
Capital City Apartments - Karen Cranford LeBeau
Connor Fitzjarrell - Stacy Hartley
Merchi Sorenson - Terra Oenning
Andrew Bronwyn - Julia Murphy and Elizabeth Ward
Sadowsky
The Filibuster - Gene Fiala

A special thank you to April Bennett and Judy Rose, my
amazing editors!

Last but not least, my family for the love and sacrifices
they have made and continue to make to help me achieve
this dream, especially my husband and best friend, Gene.
Words can never express how much you mean to me.
To our veterans and current serving members of our
armed forces, police, fire departments and EMTs, thank
you ladies and gentlemen for your hard work and
sacrifices; it's with gratitude and thankfulness that I
mention you in this forward.

DESCRIPTION

A former SEAL on a life changing mission.

A congressional aide caught up in the underworld of greed.

The explosive culmination of secrets, lies, and salvation.

Former SEAL, Creed Rowan, rescued a beautiful captive on a yacht during a mission, but there's more to his rescue than meets the eye. She's the connection RAPTOR needs to stop an international exchange and save the lives of hundreds of women.

Hope Dumond's life as a congressional aide in Washington, as ugly as it was, never prepared her for being kidnapped and within minutes of being sold as a sex slave. When her rescuer is handsome, smart, and incredibly capable of exposing those responsible, she jumps at the chance to tell him all the secrets she's uncovered. As they compile a mountain of evidence against these despicable humans, Hope longs for revenge against those responsible for trying to take her life.

Will Creed's new mission become HEALING HOPE?

Let's stay in touch where bots, algorithms and subjective admins don't decide what we see. PJ Fiala's Readers' Club is my newsletter where I promise to only send you content you enjoy! https://www.subscribepage.com/pjfialafm

GLOSSARY

Read the prequel to RAPTOR - RAPTOR Rising here. https://www.pjfiala.com/books/RR-BF

A Note from Emersyn Copeland:

Founder of RAPTOR (Revenge And Protect Team Operation Recovery).

I was wounded when my convoy hit an IED and retrained through OLA (Operation Live Again) to perform useful services for the military; mainly locating missing children. Empowered by the work but frustrated by governmental limitations, I contacted my father Dane Copeland and my Uncle Gaige Vickers, GHOST's leader, to form a covert group not restricted by governmental regulations, consisting of highly trained post military men and women with injuries and disabilities. Our offices are housed on the GHOST compound. I divided RAPTOR into three teams of expertly trained individuals who were selected for their specific abilities. Let me introduce you to the Teams.

Team Alpha: Recon and Recovery:

Diego Josephs: Former Army Recon expert. Friend of GHOST Josh Masters. Recent retraining for OLR (Operation Live Again). Demonstrative and possessive, he is a team player battling PTSD.

Ted: Diego's Therapy and service dog. A mix of black lab and Newfoundland.

Donovan "Van" Keach aka the "Reformer": Completed OLR with Emersyn. Blinded in his left eye during a military operation. Out spoken, opinionated, daredevil with a strong belief in service and a mission for justice no matter the risk.

Charlesia "Charly" Sampson: A friend of Emersyn's Aunt Sophie. Medically discharged after she lost her left arm at the elbow during a mission in Afghanistan. Tough adaptable, independent sarcastic, and determined but self-conscious of her appearance. Excels in disarming and getting people to trust her and ferreting out information.

Team Bravo: Cyber Intelligence:

Piper Dillon: Attractive and energetic with a ready smile but all business. Expert computer hacker, communications device expert and internet guru.

Caiden Marx: Strong and independent, Caiden suffered lung damage while serving due to an explosion and fire. He struggles to breathe and can't take on energetic tasks but excels on Team Bravo and has unique hacker abilities.

Deacon Smythe: Deacon has a ready smile and is always happy but takes his job seriously. He's an expert on computers and communications.

Team Charlie, Special Ops:

Falcon Montgomery: Son of Ford Montgomery, a GHOST team member, Falcon lost hearing in his right ear. Growing up with Ford, Falcon is a natural in special ops, and willing to go the extra mile to get the job done.

Creed Rowan: Former SEAL, well rounded in terms of skill, Creed's specialties are explosives and swimming. His abilities take him places others don't dare go.

Emersyn Copeland: Daughter of GHOST founder, Dane Copeland and niece to current GHOST owner, Gaige Vickers, Emersyn's strengths are in business and extracting her staff member's special talents. But, she's equally good at ferreting out suspects' deep dark secrets.

House Staff:

Sheldon Daniels, Cook: Former military, Marine. Friend of GHOST's house keeper and cook Mrs. James. Demands order in his kitchen, punctuality and the keeper of all secrets, bonus he's a damned good cook.

Shioban O'Hearn, Housekeeper: Sassy mid- thirties housekeeper. Loves the thrill of working with badasses, but doesn't let herself get walked on.

1

Falcon entered the lower cabin ahead of him and began untying the women. He heard them shushing him and his stomach knotted. They were so afraid of being found out they'd remain quiet no matter what. Falcon freed the first woman and Creed reached down into the cabin to help her up the four narrow steps to the deck. Her fingers shook and she held his hand so tightly he almost grimaced. He brought her around to the back of the boat where Emmy and Kori waited for them. She gasped and froze. The two guards they'd sedated, thanks to Kori, lay on the deck side by side, their hands and ankles tied. They'd shot them up with a sedative Kori had gotten for them and the men now blissfully slept. The third guard could now be heard thrashing in the water and Creed knew he'd need to take care of him in a few minutes.

"It's alright, they're drugged and can't hurt you."

"There's only two."

"Yes. And one in the water."

"No, you don't understand. Then you only have three of them. There are four men here."

"Shit." He hurried her along to the Jet Ski below where Emmy waited.

"These ladies will get you and the others to safety."

Creed got her on the swim platform and watched as she climbed down the ladder to Emmy's waiting Jet Ski. As soon as she was on, he looked over the side of the boat at the third guard still swimming toward them.

With Falcon's assistance, another woman emerged from below deck, so he went below deck to finish untying the last two women.

He quickly untied the third woman and then the fourth, who was still in a state of inebriation.

"She's been drugged. They don't like her." The woman said as she rubbed her wrists.

"Do you know why?"

"No. Just heard them murmuring that she wasn't going to make it."

Creed lifted the slight woman into his arms and turned to the steps. "You need to go up there. The guards we have are drugged, they won't hurt you."

The sounds of an altercation reached his ears. Falcon had engaged the final guard in a fist fight. He hurried the women to the back of the boat and helped them down.

The drugged woman needed help but, to her credit, the third woman helped her in the boat with Kori's assistance.

Creed turned his attention to the fight. The guard pulled a weapon on Falcon; Creed lunged at his legs and knocked him off-balance. His gun went off, but he then hit the side of the boat and toppled overboard.

Falcon ran toward the transom of the boat, Creed close behind him. Kori sat awkwardly in the driver's seat of their rented boat with blood spatter on her face and neck.

Falcon pulled Kori off the driver's seat and sat with her in his lap as Creed took the wheel and sped their boat out of the Gulf and toward Emmy and her Jet Ski up ahead. The two women he'd just helped into the boat huddled together and cried.

As he drove the boat, he continued to look behind to make sure the guards didn't have a way to follow them. They wouldn't bring the *Iskusheniye* because they didn't want to enter US waters. The last time he turned back he saw the guard in the water climbing the swim ladder. He wasn't sure about the guard who'd hit his head as he went over.

One last glance back and his eyes landed on the scared women at the back of the boat. He scanned to Falcon, who cradled Kori in his arms and tried to keep her calm.

As he neared Emmy's Jet Ski he slowed the boat; Falcon stood and set Kori on the seat, then made his way to the swim platform at the back to help them board.

After Falcon helped the two women onto the boat, he heard Emmy say, "Falcon, my hip is locked. I can't seem to straighten it."

Falcon jumped onto the Jet Ski behind Emmy. "Creed, I need help."

Creed shuffled back to them. "Her hip is locked. When I stand and twist, I need you to grab her in case the Jet Ski pushes away from the boat."

"Hang on." Creed climbed down the swim ladder. "Emmy, can you climb on my back?"

Falcon turned side-saddle with Emmy on his lap. "Emmy when I stand, you grab Creed with all you've got and hold on tight."

"Got it."

"One. Two. Three."

Falcon stood and Emmy grabbed his shoulders with all her might. He felt her fingers wrap themselves into his shirt and her good leg wrapped around him the best she could.

Creed leaned forward to help Emmy and crawled up onto the swim platform, then into the back of the boat. As soon as he didn't need his hands anymore to steady them, he wrapped them around Emmy's legs to hold her in place. Two of the women stood and helped steady him on the seat at the back of the boat so Emmy could sit.

Kori made her way to them. "Creed, let me take a look at her while you get Falcon on the boat and us out of here."

The adrenaline rushing through his veins kept his mind focused. He turned to see Falcon tie the Jet Ski to the back of the second one and swam toward the boat. For a man who had been shot recently, he moved with a fair amount of grace.

Creed reached down and hefted his friend onto the boat and went back to the driver's seat. "Okay, I'm taking off."

Falcon sat and watched Kori with a scowl on his face. To her credit, she didn't look up but focused her attention on Emmy.

Just as he sped them back to the marina Kori yelled out. "Falcon, call an ambulance and have them at the marina for us."

Creed focused on keeping the boat steady. They'd had no time to reassure the women that they wouldn't hurt them. But then again, somehow they knew it would be better than their situation on the boat. The wind blew over him as he navigated the buoys in the water. He sighed as he saw the marina in the distance and they'd had no encounter from behind them. But up ahead? Who knew if there were comrades on land they'd need to deal with.

Inhaling deeply and working to keep his breathing steady, he looked back again to see if they were in the clear. The women sat huddled together, the woman who'd been drugged seemed to be coming around a bit.

A quick glance at Emmy and his stomach soured. The pain on her face was palpable.

2

―――――

Her stomach felt as though it would spill right out of her any moment. It was one thing being on the much larger boat, but this one—gawd, this one moved a lot more. And the drugs in her system made her feel nauseous to begin with. She tried closing her eyes and breathing in fresh air to quell the nausea.

"Here, do you need to eat something to stave off the sickness?"

Hope opened her eyes. The woman with the bad hip held a package of crackers in her fingers.

"Thank you," she managed to say. Her fingers were so weak she had a difficult time with the package, and she ended up dropping her hands to her lap with the crackers in them. Valerie, one of her fellow victims, leaned over. "Here, let me help you."

Valerie opened it for her, pulled a cracker out of the package and lifted it to her. "You should try to nibble on this to settle your stomach. Those drugs they gave you are pretty nasty."

Hope smiled weakly and swallowed. "Thank you."

Valerie laid her arm around Hope's shoulders and held her close. It felt nice. She bit the corner off the cracker in her hand and slowly chewed it.

She opened her eyes again as the boat slowed.

Her heart pounded furiously and her fingers shook. A fresh wave of nausea threatened to erupt at the thought of what or who they'd meet at the marina. She held her stomach as it tightened and lurched.

Valerie patted her shoulder. "It's alright, we're finally to safety."

"It's not safe for me."

"What? Of course it is. There will be police there to help us."

She looked up at the man with the prosthetic leg, Creed. He turned to look at her then. Her bottom lip trembled and she shook her head slowly. "It's not safe for me. They'll have me killed." She scurried to the corner of the bench seat and wrapped her arms around herself.

He tossed a rope to someone on the dock and switched off the motor. He made his way back to her and Valerie. Valerie stood, "Can we get off the boat now?"

"Yes. Police are on the dock waiting to take your statements."

Valerie left and Creed sat in her place. She swallowed so she wouldn't throw up on him. "They'll have me killed. It's not safe for me." She locked eyes with him as she begged, "Please don't let them kill me."

"Who'll have you killed? The traffickers?"

"Yes. But they aren't who you think they are."

EMTs boarded the boat and helped Emmy onto a stretcher while she sat stone still hoping Creed or any one of them would help her.

After the EMTs left with Emmy, she noticed it was only Creed and her on the boat.

Her eyes watered and she inhaled the deepest breath she could. "Please help me."

Creed put his arm around her shoulders and pulled her close. "I'll help you. Don't worry, I won't let anyone kill you."

Tears spilled down her cheeks, but no sound came from her throat. She simply felt like a rung-out rag. "They've drugged me and it makes me very tired. But I'm petrified to fall asleep. I have no right to ask you, but will you please stay with me?"

"I promise you I will stay with you. I'm a former SEAL; honor means everything to me. If I say I'll be here while you sleep, I mean it. I'll be here until you tell me to leave."

The tears continued to track down her cheeks and a male voice startled her from her sleepiness. "Ma'am, we need to have a look at you."

She stiffened and Creed softly said into her ear, "I'm right here with you."

She swallowed and the EMT gently took her blood pressure, listened to her heart and looked at her pupils.

"Ma'am, what is your name?"

"Hope."

"Okay, Hope. Do you happen to know what drugs they were giving you?"

"No." It came out as a whisper. She licked her lips.

"Do they make you sleepy?"

She nodded.

"How about dry mouth?"

She nodded again.

"Do your limbs feel heavy?"

Nodding again, she licked her lips once more but it felt as though it did little good.

"Okay. We'd like to take you to the hospital, get the drugs out of your system and get you healthy again."

Her heart felt like it would explode and she turned to look into Creed's eyes. He must have seen the panic in hers because he shook his head. "I promise you. I promised you. I will be right there with you."

She swallowed. Creed continued. "The most important thing is to get you healthy."

"If I'm not protected, they'll have me killed. They had me kidnapped."

"Who is they, Hope?"

She turned her head to see the EMT watching her. She stared at her hands in her lap and the EMT stood. "I'll give you a couple of minutes to talk."

She felt the boat move as he stepped off onto the dock and Creed's fingers softly lifted her face to his gaze.

"Hey. Who had you kidnapped?"

"Congressman Compton and his wife."

"What? Why would they want to do that?"

"They're involved in it. The trafficking. I found out. They don't want me to tell anyone what I know."

"Holy fuck!" he muttered. She watched Creed mull this information over then he looked into her eyes again. "Do you have proof?"

She nodded but said nothing and he heaved out a deep breath. "I'll do everything I can to make sure you're safe."

A sob broke from her throat and filled her ears as Creed's arms wrapped around her and held her tight.

3

Creed picked Hope up and once the boat settled again, he took the few steps to the front where the dock was easier to reach. He lifted her toward the dock and set her down gently.

"Stay there. I'll help you."

He turned and grabbed his bag, slung it over his shoulder, then stepped onto the dock. He lifted her easily and walked toward the waiting EMT at the end of the pier.

Hope shook as he carried her and her body was stiff, the fear radiating from her.

The EMT had a gurney waiting for them and he laid Hope on it. Her hands grasped for him as they began wheeling her to the ambulance.

"You promised!"

"I did."

Creed looked at the EMT. "I need to stay with her. Will that be an issue?"

"We don't have the room, sir."

Hope sobbed and Creed turned to face the EMT. "If I can't go in the ambulance with her, I'll drive her myself to the hospital."

Indecision clear in his expression, the EMT wavered. "Let me see what we have going on."

The two of them pulled the gurney across the parking area to the ambulance and Hope's fingers gripped his hand tightly as they did. His heart hurt for her.

The EMT finished a discussion with his partner and came back to him. "We'll be able to let you ride with her in the second ambulance. The first one is full with the two women from your group."

"That's fine. We can wait."

Hope lay her head back and exhaled. The tears that tracked down her temple broke his heart. The lump that grew in his throat was difficult to swallow.

He shook his head quickly to remove the negative thoughts and reminded himself to think clearly. Hope felt she needed protection and he needed to figure out how to do that. He couldn't be with her twenty-four seven. He'd need to vet a private security firm here in the Miami area and make sure they were credible and not on the take. Though you never really knew. His best bet would be to bring Charly or Piper here.

Caiden could help too. He didn't lack for support from his RAPTOR comrades, that was for certain.

The second ambulance came rushing down the road toward them, the sirens blaring, lights flashing. Hope lifted her head at the noise then laid her head back down, but her hazel eyes locked onto his.

The fear in her eyes and her silent plea made him want to promise to wrangle the moon for her. It was both fear-inducing and awe-inspiring at the same time. He wasn't sure he'd ever have the words for it. The feelings that flushed through his body at the look in her eyes staggered him.

He squeezed her fingers to reassure her because he was afraid to speak in this moment.

Tires on the pavement close to them diverted his attention and he looked up at the EMT as she stepped from her vehicle and walked toward them.

"Hello. I understand we're bringing two passengers back with us."

He nodded. "Yes ma'am. My name's Creed Rowan and I'm Hope's protection at the moment."

"Okay, Creed. My name's Darcy Jo." She looked at Hope. "I'm going to take your vitals and then as we travel to the hospital, my partner will take over with your care as I drive us to the hospital. Creed will be allowed to stay in the back with you as we travel. Okay?"

Hope nodded, then her eyes darted to his once more.

He smiled at her and nodded once as they moved in unison toward the ambulance. Darcy Jo took Hope's blood pressure and recorded it in her unit's device, then checked her temp and eyes.

Darcy Jo then spoke softly to her. "Hope, I'll be driving the ambulance, but this is my partner, Wesley. He'll take good care of you and Creed will be right there with you the entire time. Okay?"

Hope nodded and whispered, "Okay."

Wesley took the back of the gurney and pushed it to the ambulance where a good shove collapsed the front legs and inserted the gurney into the rails in the ambulance. Another good shove and the stretcher was locked in place in the back of the ambulance. Darcy Jo squeezed Hope's ankle gently before walking to the cab.

Wesley held his hand out for Creed to precede him into the back of the ambulance and he climbed inside and scooted to the back. He laid his hand on Hope's head. "I'm here with you, Hope. I'll stay with you."

She nodded and he kept his hand there. He watched as Wesley inserted an IV into Hope's arm and explained, "This is just an IV to hydrate you, Hope. By hydrating you we're hoping to flush the drugs out of your system and get you on the mend faster. Just a little poke here."

Hope barely winced as the needle was inserted into her arm, and once Wesley had the IV in and taped down, he pounded on the side of the ambulance which was the signal for Darcy Jo to begin driving.

The ambulance swayed as they moved down the road, but nothing jarring, and he watched Hope the entire time, her words ringing in his ears at the magnitude of what was actually going on with this trafficking ring. It ran all the way to Washington and his stomach dropped at the thought of how high up this business went. Politicians were disgusting on a good day. But too many of them wielded an enormous amount of power and they were in for a rough ride with this one.

4

——————

Hope woke and sat up straight in bed. Her eyes felt heavy and unfocused but the fear that clawed inside her body demanded answers. Movement to her right startled her but his voice reassured her.

"Hey, I'm still here. I've been with you the entire time like I promised."

Her heart thrummed so fast she felt nauseous. She took in a deep breath and held it for a few moments to gather her composure.

When she opened her eyes again, he was staring back at her with a comforting expression in his deep brown eyes. His gaze held hers steady and a sense of relief washed over her before she slowly laid back in her bed and closed her eyes.

"Thank you for staying. I wasn't sure you would." She licked her parched lips.

"I told you I would, and I don't break my word."

The sound of his movement caused her to open her eyes and watch him.

He poured her a glass of water from a plastic pitcher on the bedside table. The water and ice cubes clinking against the glass as he poured sounded wonderful and her dry throat begged for the cool liquid.

"Here, take a drink." His husky voice sent a chill down her arms.

"Thank you." She sat up again, but he reached for the remote and lifted the head of her bed for her and she relaxed back into the mattress and pillow.

Her fingers shook when she took the proffered glass from his hand. When her fingers brushed his, she felt the warmth and strength there and she relaxed a bit more.

She drank the water and savored the chill as it slid down her throat. Creed's fingers pulled the cup away from her lips and her eyes flew open.

"You need to sip it or it'll upset your stomach."

"Oh. I just didn't realize just how thirsty I was until you poured it."

He smiled at her, a fascinating sight. His dark hair and dark eyes belied the paleness of his skin tone. Perhaps he spent a lot of time indoors. Yet as she studied him, she found broad shoulders connected to muscled arms. His shirt stretched tightly over a firmly defined chest. Her eyes lifted again to the even features of his face. His neatly trimmed beard fit his face perfectly, and she thought she saw the hint of a dimple in his cheek, but perhaps it was the light playing tricks on her.

"How are you feeling?" He seemed not to mind her examination, and a smile played at his full lips.

"Better. Still a little groggy, but I feel a bit stronger now."

"Good. It'll continue that way until those drugs are completely out of your system."

She nodded and continued to stare into his eyes.

He cleared his throat lightly. "Do you feel strong enough to talk about things?"

She fidgeted a bit and moved to make herself more comfortable. "Yeah."

"But it makes you nervous?"

"It does."

He turned and pulled the chair to the edge of the bed, then sat alongside. He crossed his prosthetic over his good knee, and she stared at it.

"How did you lose your leg?"

"I got shot up a little in the Middle East. It decimated my lower leg and changed my career path."

"You were a SEAL. I remember you telling me."

"Yes. I was a SEAL. But I had to leave once my leg was gone. It was for the safety of my brothers."

She nodded and swallowed the lump that instantly formed in her throat. "I'm sorry."

He shook his head. "Don't be. Everything happens for a reason. I've retrained and I work with a fantastic group of operatives now. I'm here because I'm not there."

"Makes sense."

"Can you tell me more about your situation? You mentioned Congressman Compton and his wife. I'd like to know more."

Her eyes instantly darted to the door and her back stiffened. Even the mention of their names made her body crawl with all forms of bad thoughts and reactions.

"Can you tell me what you mean by operatives? What is your group called and why did you rescue us?"

Creed planted both feet back on the floor and leaned forward with his elbows on his knees. He took a deep breath. "We're called RAPTOR. Revenge And Protect Team Operation Recover. Emmy, who you met briefly on the boat is our leader. She owns the company. We're all former military who were injured in the line of duty and had to retrain to do something different. Our main focus is rescuing trafficking victims. We do other types of work too, but this is our main focus. We get money from an agency connected to the government, to support us."

Her back stiffened and she sucked in her breath at the sound of the government.

"Hearing that distresses you." He added.

She swallowed but only nodded.

"I'm not sure what I need to do to prove I'm not here to hurt you. Tell me what proof you need and I'll get it."

"I don't know..." She swallowed again. "I don't know what that would look like."

He nodded. "Okay. Fair enough."

She picked at the threads in her blanket before looking at him. "Do you know Congressman Compton?"

"No. I don't like politicians. If I don't have to meet them, I steer clear."

She giggled slightly. "Yeah. There's so few of them who are worth a salt. That's a certainty."

"How do you know Congressman Compton?"

She swiveled her head on her shoulders and enjoyed feeling the tension ease up. "He's my...he was my boss."

"What did you do for him that you use the word was?"

"I was a congressional aide. Mostly I did research and administrative type things for him."

Creed sat back in his chair, his eyes locked on hers. "But at some point that stopped."

_____

5

She was certainly scared. No way a person could fake anything like that. But, her color was coming back and her voice was growing stronger. Maybe by tomorrow she'd be back to normal, though how would he know?

The door to her hospital room opened and a doctor walked in. He glanced quickly at him, then looked at Hope and smiled.

"Hi, Hope, I'm Doctor Alex Stafford."

"Hi." She squirmed in her bed and he stood and held out his hand.

"Hi, Doctor Stafford, I'm Creed Rowan."

The doctor smiled at him and nodded. His eyes naturally trailed down his leg then back up. "Nice to meet you Mr. Rowan. Thank you for your service."

Creed nodded and his cheeks heated slightly. He then looked at Hope, "Do you want me to step outside?"

"No!" She looked almost panicked.

He softly smiled, "Okay. If you want privacy, I can step out into the hall."

Her head was shaking before he'd finished speaking. He walked to the side of the bed and lay his hand on her shoulder. "It's alright. I'll be right here."

She smiled, though her lips shook slightly, and he stepped back and sat in his chair once again.

Doctor Stafford cleared his throat and picked up her chart. He read what he needed then hung the chart back on the foot of the bed.

"How do you feel now Hope?"

"Better."

"Okay. Tell me what better means."

She looked at him and her lips curved up slightly. "My stomach feels better. The nausea seems to have subsided. My arms and legs don't feel like they're stuck in cement anymore. My head is a bit clearer, though it feels like my thoughts are slow to come to me."

He nodded. "That's pretty good progress."

He neared the bed and held his index finger in front of her face. "Follow my finger with your eyes only."

He slowly moved his finger from one side of her face to the other and Hope followed instructions perfectly.

"Very nice. I'd like to keep you here overnight for observation. If you have any reaction to the drugs or any food we bring in, we'll be here to help you through it. But you should be able to go home tomorrow. Do you have any questions?"

Hope only shook her head but he saw the tears spring up and fall down her cheeks as the doctor turned to him and nodded. "Nice meeting you Mr. Rowan."

"Nice to meet you as well."

Creed stood and moved the two steps to Hope's bedside. He pulled a tissue from the box on the tray table next to the bed and handed it to her, then lay the box closer to her.

He watched as she swiped the tears away and dabbed at her face, then daintily blew her nose. He reached down and lifted the wastebasket from the floor and held it up so she could toss the tissue away, then set it back where it had been.

"Why does going home make you cry?"

She swallowed. "I can't go home. I won't last a day."

"Okay. So let's discuss what you know about the congressman and his wife."

She swallowed and he watched as her fingers twisted in her lap. "Okay."

Creed pulled the chair close again and sat. He reached forward and took one of her hands in his for support. "Tell me what you found out."

"They are taking money from the sale of the women."

"How do you know this for a fact?"

"First, I overheard Will...Ah, Congressman Compton, on the phone. I knew he was speaking to Anton Smith because I answered the phone when Smith called. I heard Will tell him to squash the press on the leak. His words were, 'Those fucking women were trash to begin with. We're giving them a purpose and making them useful. So what if we make money on them?' It turned my stomach."

"Do you have proof that phone call took place?"

"No, but from that time on, when Smith called..." She shifted in her bed. "I recorded the calls."

"How did you record them?"

"On my phone." She tucked a long strand of blonde hair behind her ear. "I know it's illegal to record people when they don't know they're being recorded. But what they were doing was so disgusting."

He squeezed her hand. "What did you plan to do with the recording?"

"I wasn't sure. I just thought I needed to record it in case something happened."

"Did you think you'd have someone listen to it?"

"I didn't know. I..." She looked out the window over his shoulder and stared off for a few moments. Then her eyes locked on his once again. "I just reacted without really thinking about what I'd do or what it meant."

"That's fair. Did you record other conversations?"

"Yes. Many of them."

"What did you do with those conversations?"

She inhaled deeply and let it out slowly. "I kept them on my phone for a while, then I started getting worried about all I had. So, I saved them all to an old phone I had and I hid that phone in my office at the Capitol building. I was afraid to bring them home. I thought about a locker at the bus or train station, but I started feeling like I was being followed. My feeling was if something happened to me, the first thing they'd do is ransack my apartment. I didn't want my parents to be affected by this, so I didn't take anything there. I took a book on the shelf and I hollowed part of it out and laid my phone inside and stuck it back on the shelf. I don't think anyone will ever look there."

"Okay. How did you think you'd get it back?"

"I wasn't sure about it. I just didn't want it in my possession or anywhere that my family would be harmed."

"Did you make any other copies?"

She swallowed and he watched her bite her bottom lip then lick it. "Yes. I think that's what got me in trouble. I didn't have a way to make the additional copies, so I went to an electronics store."

"Someone at the store copied everything over for you?"

"Yes."

"What did you do with those copies?"

"I never got them back. I was kidnapped two nights later."

6

Creed took a deep breath, and she watched as he processed what she'd told him. He bit the inside of his cheek then scraped his hands through his hair. She admired the beauty of his hair. It was cut short but when he moved it, the shine mesmerized her. Shiny hair always looked healthy to her. His looked thick and soft and touchable.

His eyes landed on hers and she felt the heat climb up her cheeks. He grinned and a little thrill ran through her body. She smiled in return then looked at her hands in her lap. This was no time to be flirting.

"Do you think whoever was at the electronics store called Congressman Compton and told him what you did?"

"I don't know. I know a guy named Justin called me and said he was finished with my recordings, they were on a thumb drive, and it would be three hundred dollars." She swallowed and looked at the cup of water still sitting on her bedside table. Her hand shook as she picked up the cup and took a sip. She wanted more, but the sip helped. "I needed to go to the bank and get cash. I didn't want my card to be traced. I told him it would be a couple of days before I could get there, and he said no problem."

"And that was the last you heard from Justin?"

"Yes."

"I'd like the name of that electronics store."

Her lips frowned on their own and she knew he was confused by this because he cocked his head to the right slightly.

She swallowed and inhaled. "Byte Me. It's on East Twenty First Street in Old Town."

"Full disclosure, I'll be sending a team to check out Byte Me and Justin."

She nodded but wondered what that meant. Justin very likely almost got her killed. Trafficked at a minimum so she didn't give two shits what happened to Justin. But, she did still wonder.

"So did you go to the bank?"

Shaking her head she inhaled a deep breath. "I never made it. The day Justin called I was super busy at work, and I had dinner at my parents' that evening. I was going to go the following day to the bank, but Congressman Compton asked me to take on a couple of extra projects. I ended up working late that night getting the projects finished and went straight home afterwards."

Her bottom lip trembled and she swallowed multiple times as she struggled to breathe.

"I was taken that night."

"Where were you when you were taken?"

She cleared her throat, more to give herself time than anything else. She'd thought about it every day since she'd been taken and every time it brought her to tears. She wondered if she'd ever be able to think about any of the things that happened to her without crying ever again. "My home. They broke into my apartment. I didn't hear them."

Tears spilled from her eyes, and she let a sob rush from her body, covering her face with her hands. She jumped when she felt Creed's arms wrap around her.

He pulled back. "I'm sorry."

Then she cried again and shook her head.

He sat on her bed near her legs, facing her, and laid his hand on her knee. He said nothing but watched as she cried, heaving sobs escaped her chest. She felt for the tissue box he'd set next to her hip on the bed; she pulled several tissues and began blowing her nose. The gobs of snot and tears she cried out were enormous, at least they felt that way. After she'd cried herself out, she took several deep cleansing breaths and lay her head against her pillow until she regained her composure.

It felt like a long time. Maybe she'd even dozed off. But when she opened her eyes, he was there. Sitting still as can be in the same spot he'd sat while she cried. His hand still lay on her leg.

"You're like a sentinel."

He chuckled. "Most sentinels don't have a prosthetic leg or a quirky sense of humor."

"I didn't know you had a quirky sense of humor."

He shrugged but said nothing else. The fingers of his right hand nervously rubbed the fabric of his tactical pants.

"You're my sentinel and I don't see that your prosthetic leg keeps you from much."

His cheeks colored slightly, and she thought he was even more handsome than before, if that were possible.

"I trained and worked very hard to keep my leg from stopping me. I prefer to surprise people with my ability rather than my differing ability." His smile widened and she smiled in return. It felt good to smile again, even if only fleeting.

He cleared his throat lightly, then started again. "I'm sorry I have to ask but...you didn't hear them come into your home?"

She shook her head no, but the tears didn't come this time.

"When did you know they were there?"

"When they were in my bedroom. There were two of them. One put a rag over my face. I kicked and thrashed but that's all I remember. When I woke up, I was on a boat."

"The same boat we rescued you from?"

"No. It was smaller. It rocked a lot. I was tied to a handle on the wall, under the bow of the boat. It had a small cabin area. A bed and a table. At first I was on the bed, my hands tied together." She looked down at the bandages on her wrists and winced. "Then they tied my hands to the handle on the wall."

He nodded and his hand squeezed her leg lightly. She guessed for reassurance.

"Do you recall how long you were on that boat?"

"Only until we reached another larger boat. I was transferred to the other one. I was told if I tried anything they'd drug me again and I was more afraid of that than anything, so I went along with being moved."

"Was it dark outside?"

"Yes. Impossibly dark. The only light was from the small flashlights they used."

"Do you recall how you got on the boat? The trip from Washington to Miami?"

She cocked her head to the left and bunched her forehead up as if that would help her remember. She had no recollection of any travel or transport and that made her skin crawl. "No."

"Did we rescue you from the same boat you had been transferred to?"

"No. I was moved again a few days later." Her gaze flashed to his. "What's the date?"

"It's September twenty-ninth."

She gasped. "My God. I've been gone since September thirteenth."

"Sixteen days."

She swallowed the bile that threatened to rise in her throat. "Do you know my parents? Can I call them?"

"I don't know your parents, but you can call them. I'd like to get you a burner phone to call them with though. We'll have to assume their phones are bugged. So you shouldn't say where you are. No locations. Not right now. I can send a team out to your parents' house to check for bugs before we let them know where you are."

"They'll be so worried."

"I can only imagine. I'll need to go back to my rental and get you the burner phone."

She started shaking her head before he'd finished. "No, I'm not safe. Please don't leave me."

He held his hand up to stave off her concerns. "I've taken care of that. We've called in one of our teammates and she'll relieve me so I can rest and gather supplies. Then I'll be back soon."

"Who is that?"

"Her name is Charly. You'll love her. Everyone does."

Her breathing sped up and she laid her hand over her chest in an effort to keep her heart from exploding out of it. Her heartbeat was so rapid it made her nauseous.

7

The fear on her face as he watched her bruised his heart a bit. He didn't know the first thing about this kind of fear. He reached for her hand and squeezed it.

"I'll stay here until you meet her. I'll only be gone for a little while. I promise to be back before bedtime with a phone you can use. And I'll be here as much as I can. I'm doing this for you. Not to hurt you."

A single tear slid down her cheek and he swiped it away.

"I'm trying to do what I can for you. But, Hope, I have to leave this room sometimes. But I won't do it unless you have someone else here to be your security. I need you to understand that."

Her eyes, those gorgeous shiny brown eyes looked into his and mesmerized him. When she finally spoke to him, her voice was soft. "I understand. I just needed a minute to get my head around you not being here."

"Not being here for a *little while*. I'll be back."

"Right."

The door opened and a pretty woman with curly blonde hair and bright blue eyes, wearing tan khakis and a white three-button placket shirt walked into the room. She smiled, "Hey there, Creed." She looked at Hope, "You must be Hope, I'm Charly. I work with Creed, Falcon, and Emmy."

Hope reached forward and placed her right hand in Charly's. "Hi. Hope Dumond."

"It's nice to meet you, Hope." Charly turned to him and smiled. "Nice work on the rescue. I'm a bit irritated I wasn't here for it. But I'm stoked I'm here now. We're going to get those bastards."

"We're close Charly. So close. Hope has been offering up some great information on it."

Charly turned to Hope, "That's fantastic. I don't know how much Creed has shared with you, but we've been after this ring for a while now. It's beginning to get under our skin that it's taken us this long, but we're determined."

Hope's eyes locked on Charly's and he tried to determine if she was enchanted by Charly or unsure.

"He hasn't shared that much. I've been a bit out of it. My brain is beginning to function normally again. I think. I still feel weak and tired, but stronger. If that makes sense."

Creed grinned at her and when her eyes swung to his, he couldn't help but notice a few things about her. Her hair was dark brown but held tones of reds and auburn in it.

Her eyes were deep brown and he'd describe them as intelligent. She missed very little around her and he wasn't sure if that was a product of her recent ordeal or if she'd always been alert. If she were a congressional aide, she'd very well have to be smart. She was slight of frame and right now a bit malnourished. But that would change in a week or two with nutritious food and drink to help her regain her proper weight and strength.

Creed stood and watched Hope's face. He looked at his phone. "It's almost lunch time now. They'll be bringing you something to eat soon and if you're tired after, you should rest. Do you want Charly to stay in your room or outside?"

"In here is good."

He looked at Charly and nodded. Suddenly he was at a loss. He felt like walking out was abrupt, but he surely wouldn't hug her or kiss her goodbye or anything similar. His irritation with himself at this line of thinking had him squaring his shoulders.

"Okay, I'll get out of here. I'm going to the house to eat, grab a shower and a phone for you, and make some arrangements for tomorrow. You're in good hands with Charly. I'll set up the call with your parents as well and I'll be back here before they bring you dinner. Deal?"

Hope smiled and nodded. "Deal."

"Charly, I'm going to have Piper and Deacon run some bug checks on Hope's parents' phones before they speak. And Emmy is down the hall, so when I get back you should stop in."

Charly laughed at him. "Creed, I've already seen Emmy and you don't need to worry, I'll take good care of Hope. Do what you need to do. And, I second the shower."

His brows furrowed and he turned to see Hope grinning at him. He felt strange and awkward suddenly.

He slipped out the door and into the hall of the hospital where the food carts were being pushed down the hall, the smell of hospital chicken and canned peas filled the air. He'd had plenty of that food when he'd lost his leg and the smell of it almost made his stomach turn.

Holding his breath as he walked down the hall, he let it out when he reached the elevator, relieved when he stepped in that it didn't hold that same odor. Not that hospital food was bad, but it did churn up powerful memories and he could live without them.

He let out a long breath and mentally made his to-do list for his brief time out of the hospital. He didn't think the house was a place to bring Hope to, and he thought perhaps the hotel Emmy had the other women stay at would be a better choice, since they'd have protection there and his team wouldn't be split in protection detail. They had security and the upper floors were hard to get to if you didn't have the card for that floor. And, if the other women were there as well, Hope wouldn't be alone when he needed to leave and get some sleep. And of course, Charly was here to help now.

As he drove to the house, his phone rang. Emmy's name on the screen gave him a sense of relief.

"Hey, Emmy. How are you doing?"

"I'm fine. Doctors say I'll be home tomorrow."

"That's fantastic. I just left the hospital. I should have stopped in. I'm sorry."

"Don't be. I've mostly been sleeping. But the Miami police chief just called and they'll be releasing the women. They're scared of course and don't know what to do. I thought I'd secure the hotel where Kori's girls stayed, and they can have a day to decompress before they go home."

"I was going to talk to you about that. Hope is being released tomorrow and she's scared. Emmy, she has dirt on the congressman and his wife and Smith. That's why she was taken. They know she knows and she's in danger. We're going to need to head to Washington DC and get the proof of the players in high places to bring them all down."

8

Hope took a deep breath as Creed disappeared into the hallway. Her eyes landed on Charly who watched her closely and the gooseflesh rose on her arms.

She swallowed, "You should sit down."

Charly's lips curved up in a pretty smile and she winked. "I'm just fine and I just got off the plane about an hour ago. If you don't mind I'll stand for a bit more. If you're tired though, please lay back and rest. I'll be here. You're safe in my hands. Well, hand and this." She held up her left arm and Hope looked closely.

"Is that a prosthetic arm?"

Charly twisted her hand to and fro then grinned. "Yep. But I can do most anything with it."

"Are you all..." She stopped not sure how to ask.

"Wounded? Different? Damaged?"

"I wouldn't say damaged. But I was going to say wounded."

"Yep. We all have some differing abilities. That's how we came together. We all were entered into a retraining program to teach us to ferret out and capture pedophiles and traffickers and save those who've been caught up in their nasty dealings."

Hope looked from Charly's arm to her eyes and then back to her arm. "Wow."

Charly nodded. "Get some rest Hope. It'll help you heal up."

Hope laid her head against the pillow, but she remained in an upright position. She was nervous. Falling asleep would render her vulnerable and she had had enough of feeling vulnerable over the past sixteen days. She wondered about her parents. She wanted to speak with them so badly and let them know she was alive. Did they know that? Did they think she was dead? They must be so worried.

Tears sprang to her eyes and she blinked rapidly to dry them. Hoping it wouldn't be much longer before she could think about what happened to her and not cry. She wanted to feel strong again.

The door to her room opened and a nurse came in carrying a food tray. Her stomach growled at the wafting aroma.

The nurse giggled. "See, you're hungry. This will help you feel better. Get some nourishment in you and some sleep and you'll be right as rain in no time."

"Thank you."

The nurse laid the tray on the rolling cart to her right, then pushed the cart over the bed in front of her. Hope raised the bed a bit more so she could eat without spilling on herself and the nurse pulled the plastic top off her food. "I'll lay this on the table over here in case you want to cover it up. But, the condensation gets everything wet, so I don't want to keep it on your tray."

"Thank you."

"I have milk or apple juice, what's your preference? You can have both if you like."

Hope smiled, "Apple juice please."

"Apple juice it is. I'll be right back."

The nurse walked past Charly and ducked out the door. She returned quickly with a carton of apple juice and Hope opened the wrapper her plasticware was sealed in. The chicken looked good and it smelled good too. It had been sixteen days since she'd had a meal. A real meal. Dinner at her parents' had been her last good meal. Hopefully soon she'd be eating with her parents again.

"If you need anything just buzz me." Her nurse said.

"Thank you."

She hadn't even thought to look at her name badge and get her name, Hope thought with remorse. She'd need to brush up on her manners soon. She'd gotten so used to not looking at anyone coming or going, to staying invisible, that she'd forgotten general niceties.

She dipped her fork into the mashed potatoes on her plate and put them in her mouth. They weren't real potatoes for certain, but they tasted like food and not a meal bar. Lord she never wanted to eat a meal bar ever again. She opened a pat of butter from the side of her tray and dropped it onto her potatoes. Everything tasted better with butter. While that melted, she pulled some meat from her chicken and enjoyed the taste of it. She ate slowly, knowing her stomach would fill quickly, and she wanted to enjoy the little bit of food she could take in.

A forkful of corn, then a bit of chicken, then buttery potatoes and she was almost full. She picked up her apple juice and sipped from the tiny straw inserted into the top of it.

She managed a couple more bites of food and then lay back against her pillow.

Charly asked, "Do you want me to cover that up for you in case you can eat in a little bit?"

So, she *was* watching. "If you don't mind, I'd appreciate it."

Without a sound, Charly padded to her bedside table and pulled it slightly away. "I'll leave it within reach for you."

"I appreciate that."

Her eyes were kind and they didn't miss much. They landed on her wrists and her lips hardened before she turned and walked to a chair close to the door and finally sat.

"Have you had to protect other trafficking victims?"

Charly nodded and took a deep breath. "It was last year; police recovered five women from a warehouse where they were being held. We were there to help keep them safe until they could return home."

Hope's nose tingled and her eyes filled with tears once again. "Thank you." She managed to say before a sob escaped her throat.

She took a deep breath and let it out in a whoosh. "I hate being a baby."

Charly leaned slightly forward in her chair. "I don't think you're a baby. You've been traumatized. That will take a bit of time to overcome. You need to give yourself permission to take that time."

Hope nodded. "Thank you."

Charly smiled, then sat back in her chair. "If you need to rest, I'll be right here. No one will hurt you while I'm on the job."

Hope looked into her eyes for a long time. Charly's eyes were a light blue and her hair was the cutest curly style. It was then she wondered what her own hair looked like. It had been days since she'd showered. Even then she was only allowed five minutes and she could tell she didn't get all the soap out of it before they shut off the water.

"Thank you."

Lifting the control for the bed, she lowered the head of her bed slightly, then turned to face the door, tucking her hands under her chin and allowed her eyes to close. The soft murmur of voices outside her room lulled her to sleep.

9

Creed showered, changed clothes, and packed a bag for tomorrow in case he didn't get back here to change.

He left his bedroom and found Falcon at the stove cooking something delicious. "What are you making?"

"I'm grilling tonight. Will you be around?"

"Likely not until later if at all. I'll grab something on my way to the hospital. Leave me some leftovers though."

"Sounds good. How's Hope?"

"She's scared out of her wits. She has dirt on Congressman Compton and his wife. It's back in Washington. I think we'll be leaving to head to DC to find her evidence and bring those bastards down for good. Right from the top."

"I'm up for that. This has been a long fucking mission but we're so close now I don't want to give up on it."

"I'm right there with you."

"You going back to the hospital now?"

"Yeah, I came to get Hope a burner phone so she can call her parents. Showered, changed, and uploaded my findings to the system."

"I'll look it over while Kori sleeps. Anything you need me to do now?"

Creed looked at his teammate and smiled. "Yeah. Get some rest, you look beat."

Falcon flipped him the bird and Creed laughed as he walked out the door.

As he drove to the hospital he thought about the information they had so far on this group. They'd known for years that Dildo was dirty, but until a few months ago, they didn't know how high up his connections went. Creed was almost a little sorry Dildo was dead; if they could've gotten more information out of him they'd maybe have an easier time getting at the people in charge. He was disgusted to know it went as high as Washington politicians and it made his stomach turn. Politicians involved in something this vulgar was beyond anything he could have dreamed of. Fucking assholes preying on the people who elect them. No lower form of scum out there.

He pulled into a drive-thru and ordered the healthiest thing on the menu, which wasn't that healthy, but food just the same. He ate while he drove and tried to get his bearings about what needed to be done next.

He walked into the hospital with his duffle hanging over his shoulder and took a deep breath before he got up to the floor where Emmy and Hope were. His stomach twisted once again at the odors of antiseptic and medicines and hospital food.

The elevator stopped on the third floor. "Excuse me please." He gently moved his body forward, careful not to hit anyone with his duffle bag.

He softly knocked on Emmy's closed door and was about to leave when her voice called out, "Come in."

Pushing the door open, he stepped inside. Emmy lay on her bed, looking small and somewhat helpless.

"Hey, how are you today?"

She situated herself and pressed the button on the controller to raise her head up. "I'm good. Better than yesterday thank God."

"That's good. Is there anything you need? Hope is down the hall and to the left, so I can bring you something and run between the rooms."

She giggled. "No, I'm fine. I'm surprisingly enjoying the bit of downtime."

"Is everything going to be alright?"

"It is for now. I honestly don't know what will happen in the future, Creed. I may very well be in a wheelchair if my leg deteriorates further. But I'm not dwelling on that. I have faith everything will work out the way it's supposed to."

"I'm glad you have faith. For the record, when I lost my leg..." He looked down then back to her, "I felt angry with the world. Then I was told by my CO that I couldn't remain a SEAL and I got angrier. I only say that so you know it's alright to be angry."

Emmy smiled and nodded. "Oh, I'm all of that Creed. But, it won't serve me very well in recovery, so I'll reserve it for after we get these bastards off the streets."

"Understandable. But, you do need to be mindful of your health, Emmy."

"Yes, Dad. Please spare me the lecture; both of my parents have given it to me already. I'll be mindful and still get the job done. I won't let any of you down."

Creed inhaled a deep breath and cleared his throat. "Okay, I'll save the lecture. But we all work together in this. That means when one of us is down, the others pick up the slack. We all do this for each other. That's what a team is."

Emmy smiled at him. "And I'm honored to be with the best team on the planet."

Well, that kind of teared him up. He cleared his throat once again. "If you need anything, Emmy, please let me know."

"I will. Now, can we talk a bit of business?"

"Sure. Downtime is over?"

"For now."

"Okay. I saw Charly earlier and she's solid and ready. She'll also be a bit of a calming influence on Hope if she needs it."

"I agree."

"Also, I need to make sure you and Falcon don't burn out."

"I can handle it. Falcon has enough to do with Kori right now, and since we're wrapping up here in Miami, I feel it's important to get to Washington as soon as we can."

Emmy nodded. "I have a call in to Roxanne Delany to see about using her house as a base camp once again. GHOST used it before, and Gaige said it worked out wonderfully. I think that will be our course of action for now. We can keep Hope safe there if she needs the protection."

"She does. She's scared shitless, Em. She said the congressman had her kidnapped because he found out she'd been recording him. She has the recordings hidden. Though it may well be a bitch to get them, we have to try. This goes too high up to let it alone."

Emmy nodded. "Okay. Keep us posted on any information you get from her for now. When is she being released?"

"In the morning."

"Okay. Will she be going to the hotel?"

"Yes. I don't think the house is secure enough right now. Unless you hear from Roxanne first, then I'd like us to head there right away."

10

The door to her room opened and Creed stepped inside. She didn't want to admit to herself how happy she was that he was back.

"Hey, there. You look rested."

She smiled and her cheeks heated. "Thank you. I did take a nap and I ate some food."

"Ahh, that's great. That's how you'll get stronger."

Creed then turned Charly. "Any problems?"

"No, none."

"Good. Emmy says you'll be going to the hotel with the women as soon as they're released from the police department."

"Yes. I'll be picking them up as soon as they call."

"Thank you for helping us with this."

"It's my pleasure. Have you spoken to Emmy?"

"Yes. She has a call in to Roxanne Delany and we'll head there as soon as we have the okay."

"Great. I'll be ready. I'll update myself on everything as soon as I get the women to the hotel. Have you updated?"

"I did."

"Okay. I'll see you both a bit later. Nice meeting you Hope."

"Thank you, Charly. It was nice meeting you too."

He stopped at the chair he'd sat in earlier and dropped his duffle bag in the seat. He reached inside and pulled out a small box. He worked at the packaging, and she watched his fingers as they deftly opened the plastic covering, then the box, and pulled out a phone.

"This is a burner phone for you to use. There are rules." He powered the phone up and waited for a signal. He pulled his phone out of the pocket of his tan khakis and held it next to the burner phone. "I'm downloading some phone numbers. Mine. Falcon's. Charly's. Emmy's and headquarters. If you can't get the four of us here, you can call headquarters, and someone will be able to assist you."

"Okay. Thank you."

"Also—" he tapped on her phone and his fingers worked on the screen, though she couldn't see what he was doing. "You can call your parents, but as I mentioned before you can't tell them where you are. We're trying to find out if their phone is bugged. We have equipment we can use to scan their phone while we're talking to them. So you can tell them to expect a call from Piper, Deacon, or Caiden."

"Okay. Piper, Deacon, or Caiden."

"Correct. You can't tell them you'll be home soon until one of my team has managed to call them and scan their phone."

"Okay. They'll ask. What should I say?"

"Tell them once they receive a call you'll be able to tell them a bit more. Just that you're safe for right now."

"I need to tell them to be careful."

"No. Once we've made sure their phones aren't bugged, we can let them know more. For right now tell them you're sorry you can't give them more information but for security reasons it will have to be good enough to know you're fine."

"They'll be happy to know that."

He handed her the phone, but he held on to it and she looked up into his eyes. "No funny business, Hope. This is for your protection."

She swallowed and those pesky tears filled her eyes. She swallowed profusely and nodded. "I won't say anything."

He smiled and her lips turned up into a smile. "Thank you."

He nodded. "Of course. Do you want me to leave the room?"

"No." She said it quickly and then blushed. "Um, no. Do you mind staying?"

Shaking his head, he took a deep breath and sat in the chair Charly had vacated, though he moved it closer to her. She dialed her mom's number, though it took a while. Her fingers shook terribly.

Her mom's soft voice answered, "Hello?"

A sob came from her throat before she could say a word. "Mom?" Her voice shook and the tears streamed down her cheeks.

Creed moved the tissue box to her tray table then sat back down.

"Oh my God. Hope? Hope, honey, is that you?"

She sniffed and swiped at her nose with a tissue she'd pulled from the box. "Yes," she said softly.

"Ohhh." Her mom's sob on the other end of the line caused Hope to cry once more. She held the phone with both of her hands. Her fingers shook so badly she was afraid she'd drop it and disconnect.

"Where are you, baby?"

Hope sniffed and took a deep breath. "I can't tell you that yet, Mom."

Her mom's voice shook. "Are you alright?"

Hope cleared her throat and took a deep breath. "I am now. I'm safe. I'm protected." Her eyes darted to Creed and he smiled at her.

Her mom blew her nose and sniffed. "When can I see you?"

"It'll be a while, Mom. But I promise as soon as I can tell you I will."

Her mom let out a long breath. "I have to sit down." She heard a chair scrape on the floor and in her mind she pictured the kitchen table and the chair, her mom's favorite chair facing the back yard. Picturing her mom sitting in that chair now made her heartbeat speed up and her stomach tightened. Oh, what she wouldn't give to hug her mom right now.

"Are you alright, Mom?"

Sniffing and the sound of a tissue moving against the microphone on her phone came across first then her mom's soft voice. "I am. I'm just so...haaappy..." Her mom sobbed again, and Hope closed her eyes.

"Mom. I promise you I'll explain everything to you soon. But for now, please know I'm safe. I'm protected and I miss you so fucking much."

"Hope!"

"Don't be mad. It's the strongest word I could think of right now. I love you and Daddy so damned much and I miss you both."

Her mom let out a breath, "Oh honey. We've been so worried. We've been doing everything we can to keep your picture on the news. We miss you, too. We want you back."

"I'll be back."

Her mom sobbed again and Hope sat and listened. Her tears had dried up and now all she could think of was to get the bastards that had put her parents through this.

"Is Daddy home?"

Sniffing. "No honey, he had to go to work."

Hope pulled her phone screen from her ear and looked at the time. "Why did he go to work so late?"

"Ah, he hasn't been going in every day. We've been looking for you. But he needed to handle a few things and this is a good time of the day to do it."

"Okay. Mom, listen. You'll be receiving a phone call from either Piper, Caiden, or Deacon. They will be able to give you a little more information, but you need to listen to them and do as they ask."

"Oh my God, are you being held captive?"

"No." She cleared her throat. "No, mom, I'm fine. I promise you. But they are helping me stay safe. So, they will call you soon and you need to follow their directions. Okay?"

11

———

Creed listened to Hope talk to her mom, and he was proud of her. She did as he asked and she did it well.

They talked about little things. How is the dog? How is her brother? Did her dad get that new suit he was hesitating on? Mundane things.

When she finished her call, she held the phone to her chest for a long time as if she were hugging her mom. He cleared his throat, "Are you alright?"

Hope's eyes opened and landed on him. The look on her face made him think she'd forgotten he was there.

"Yes. I..." She cleared her throat. "I'm taken by surprise at how emotional that was."

Creed nodded his head. "Yeah. I'll have you together with them as soon as we can."

She inhaled and let it out slowly then settled her body into her bed. Though she still sat up he saw her body relax.

"I'm sorry you can't say anything to them just yet."

She scoffed. "No one knows more than I do the danger that could befall them if they knew what I know. I don't want them in harm's way for any reason at all. Certainly not because of me."

Creed nodded. "I'm happy you feel that way."

The door opened and a nurse walked in with a food tray. As she lifted the lid covering the plate of food, Creed held his breath until the nurse left. Slowly, he let his breath out and took shallow breaths so as not to smell the food completely.

Hope hesitated as she picked up her fork, "Did you eat something today?"

"I ate on the way here. Go ahead, please."

He saw her throat constrict as she swallowed then, she opened the plastic pouch that held her plasticware and moved the food around on her plate. It looked like meat-loaf, though he tried not to stare at it. Instead, he pulled his phone out and texted Emmy.

"Hope called her parents. She didn't tell them where she is."

Emmy responded rather quickly and he wondered if she'd gotten her food yet or if she'd already finished.

"Good. Charly has the women at the hotel."

He nodded, sent Emmy a thumbs up and texted Cyber team. "Hope called her mom. She's waiting for a call from one of you."

Caiden sent a thumbs up and he tucked his phone into the side pocket of his khakis. When he looked at Hope she was watching him and his stomach tightened. She was pretty. Her color was coming back and there was a soft pink in her cheeks. The brown of her eyes made the white around the colored iris look whiter. She had a gorgeous smile, at least the one or two times he'd seen it, and it left an impression on him.

"Is everything alright?"

His eyes focused on hers once more. "Yes. I'm sorry, did it look like something was wrong?"

"Yes. Your brows are furrowed."

Shaking his head quickly, he sat up straighter in the chair, laid his elbows on the arms, and folded his hands in front of him. "Sorry. My mind never stops thinking. It's like that for most of us at RAPTOR. We need to constantly think and rethink to make sure we've covered all of the bases. Sometimes, one wrong move can have dire consequences."

She laid her fork alongside her plate and folded her hands on her lap. "Are you telling me the truth about being safe here?"

"Yes." He cleared his throat. "We can't guarantee anything of course. But, I'm here and my team is taking all the precautions it can. For right now, we don't know who is working for the congressman or Smith so nothing is one hundred percent. But I'm here to protect you if you need it, and if I have to be gone for a while, we have Charly or Falcon to rely on. Emmy said if we need it, she'll bring more team members here, but I think we all need to head to Washington."

Hope's eyes rounded. He held up a hand. "I know, you are worried about safety. We're working on that now. We have a home to stay in that belongs to a sister team member's spouse. We can more easily protect you there. That house is secured beautifully."

Hope nodded. "I'm scared out of my wits to be honest. But I'm also mad as hell. I'm so sickened by what Compton, his wife, Helen, and Smith are doing to innocent people. Women they so easily decide aren't worthy of living a good life. I heard them called throwaways, losers, miscreants, lowlifes, and so many other derogatory names. They don't get to decide who can turn their lives around and who can't. And they sure as hell don't get to take my life or anyone else's because I know what disgusting behavior they're engaged in."

"I'm sure they are terrified of what you know. And, by now, we have to assume they know you've been rescued."

"Is it safe for me to stay here? Will they assume I've been brought to the hospital?"

"It's the question I've been asking myself."

Hope pushed her tray table away from her. "Can I go to the hotel tonight? That way you won't be divided up for protection. Maybe you can get the doctor to release me. If they have access to hospital records they'll know I'm here."

"I can check with the doctor. Kori is an EMT, so if we need something she could help."

"She got shot."

"It isn't bad, as wounds go. She's battling fatigue more than anything else at this point."

Hope pulled her covers back and twisted so her feet dangled from the bed. "I really don't want to stay here. Can you see if you can pull some strings?"

12

Hope pushed the button on the controller laying on her bed. She waited for the nurse to come in and her heart beat rapidly as she tried pushing thoughts away about just how vulnerable she was here. She'd never let herself be taken again. She'd kill herself before that would happen. She'd listened as the women she was with shared their stories of forced prostitution and the houses of horrors they lived in.

The door opened and a nurse, whose name badge said Julie, with happy face stickers surrounding her name, entered her room.

"How can I help you Hope?"

"I want to leave."

"But the doctor wanted to keep you overnight for observation."

Hope looked Julie in the eyes. "I'm not safe here. The people who kidnapped me are very connected and the fact that there are hospital records with my name and location on them makes me a sitting duck here."

"But, those records aren't public sweetie."

"The people who are after me don't need the records to be public. They have ways of getting into your systems and ferreting out information. The fact that by now they know I've been rescued has put a target on my back."

"Oh, honey, the drugs are making you feel para..."

"No!"

Julie straightened and Creed stood and walked to her bedside.

"She's not paranoid. She's correct. That's why I'm here and another security professional was here earlier today."

"Oh." Julie looked into her eyes once again and tried to smile, but it didn't reach her eyes. "I'll see if I can get ahold of your doctor."

Hope stood, pulling her hospital issued gown around her backside and checking that she was covered.

"Even if you can't get ahold of him, I'm leaving here. I'd prefer to do it correctly, but I'm not staying here."

Julie nodded then turned and left the room.

Hope padded to the closet cabinet across her room. She pulled her clothing from inside, which the nurse had folded and laid in the drawer, but the smell nauseated her the instant the drawer opened.

Turning to Creed he nodded. "I have a T-shirt and sweatpants you can wear. I'm certain they'll be too big for you, but it's temporary. I'll see if someone can go shopping to get you some clothing."

"Thank you."

Creed walked to his duffle still sitting on a chair and unzipped the top. He pulled out a neatly folded gray T-shirt and pair of navy sweatpants. He turned to hand them to her. "I have a pair of underwear if you need them."

Her face burned hot and her stomach twisted. "No. I'll pass. But, thank you."

He nodded and she turned to make her way to the bathroom to change.

Just as she pulled the T-shirt over her head she heard the door to her room open and Creed speaking with someone. She froze and listened to the conversation and realized it was her doctor and the nurse who conversed with him.

Turning to the mirror, she finger-combed her hair, brushed her teeth, and exited the bathroom.

Her doctor turned toward her as she entered the room and nodded. "I understand you intend to leave this evening."

Nodding, "Yes. Actually, right now."

Her doctor looked down at her chart and heaved out a deep breath.

"Keeping you here is a formality to ensure you don't have issues from the drugs in your system. But I do understand your security risk and it's better for your mental health that you feel safe, which also impacts your physical health. I'll sign your discharge paperwork immediately and Julie will take care of the release for you."

Hope's eyes darted to Creed's, which stared back at her. His lips turned up into a soft smile and she instantly felt better. Turning to her doctor once more she nodded. "Thank you. Please know I'm not trying to be harsh or a pain, but I don't feel safe here. There are simply too many people running around that can be bought. I won't allow myself to be taken. Not ever again."

"I can't say that I know personally what you mean, but I do understand your need for safety."

He turned and left the room, Julie following him out the door.

Hope took a deep cleansing breath and let it out slowly. Now just to get out of here.

"Thank you for helping me with them."

Creed smiled at her. This time it was a genuine smile. "I'm happy to do it." He looked at her tray table and asked, "What do you need to pack up?"

Hope looked at the drawer her filthy clothing lay in, then shook her head. "I'll just grab my hospital issue tooth-brush and toothpaste. That's it."

"Are you sure? We can wash your clothes."

"No. I never want to see those clothes again. I've been in them for sixteen days. The memories they hold are nauseating."

Creed walked to the closet and opened the door. Bending down he pulled her shoes from the floor. "You'll have to wear these I'm afraid. At least until we can get you something else."

She looked at her shoes as he carried them to the side of the bed. "I can live with that."

Her feet were silent on the cold tile floor as she neared her bed. She pinched the material of the leg of Creed's borrowed sweatpants to lift the bottom so she could slip her foot into her ballerina flats. Repeating the motion on the other leg, she stood and caught Creed's gaze as he stared at her.

"What?"

He chuckled. "My clothes look good on you."

She shrugged. "They're actually not bad." She lifted her shirt slightly to show him the waistband. "There's a string here to tighten the waist." Dropping the T-shirt she then gathered the material at the right side and twisted it into a knot. "And now, I'm a fashion statement."

Creed laughed and nodded and she couldn't look away from him. "That you are."

Nurse Julie entered the room with a handful of papers. "Sorry, but you need to sign your voluntary discharge papers, Hope."

Hope sat on the edge of the bed and pulled the hospital tray toward her. Julie laid the papers on the top and one by one, explained what she was signing and then flipped the page to expose one more paper.

13

The nurse brought in a wheelchair and Hope shook her head.

"I don't want to use that."

"I'm sorry, it's policy."

"I'll sign a paper saying I'm responsible. I need to stay close to Creed."

The nurse took a deep breath and straightened her shoulders. "I'll see what the doctor says."

He looked at her face, so filled with fear. "Let's just go. It's not like they can really do anything about it."

She moved off the bed and he held his hand out to her. He picked up his duffle, in which he'd also placed the few things she had with her inside, and he escorted her out the door of her hospital room.

They passed the nurses station and headed to the bank of elevators at the far end of the lobby. He pushed the button on the wall to summon the elevator and watched Hope turn her head to and fro.

"It's okay, Hope. I'm here with you."

Her fingers tightened in his hand, and she let out a breath but said nothing.

The doors opened and three women emerged from the elevator. Hope stiffened alongside him, and he squeezed her hand in reassurance. At least he hoped that's what he conveyed.

They stepped inside and he pushed the button for the first floor, then the close-door button, to get them rolling down to the lobby. Unfortunately, the elevator stopped at the third floor and as soon as the doors opened, two large men stepped inside.

Hope pushed into his side, and actually tried to step behind him to shield herself and his heart hurt for her.

Creed stopped the doors from closing and pulled Hope from the elevator. They stood to the side of the elevator when one of the men stepped from the elevator and faced them.

Hope let out a half-scream-half-cry and started to run. Creed grabbed her arms and held her, then shielded her with his body as the man took three menacing steps toward them.

"It's him. The man who was in my apartment. He had a limp."

Creed grabbed Hope's hand and took off running toward the nurses' station. The man followed them, though he did have a limp and it slowed him down. As they reached the nurses' station he yelled, "Call the police. Kidnapper on the floor."

The nurse who had checked Hope out, looked behind him at the man running toward them and Creed pulled Hope along and around a corner. He heard a commotion behind them and knew that the nurses managed to slow down the man following them.

Creed ducked into an empty office and tucked Hope behind the door. "Stay here. Stay down."

"Don't leave me."

"I'm not going anywhere, but I'm not letting him get away. Whatever happens, you stay right there. Police are on the way."

He cracked the door open and heard things crashing. Glancing at Hope, he shook his head. "Stay right here so I know where to find you. Lock the door when I step out."

"Please don..."

"Lock. The. Door."

He stepped out and waited to hear the lock click in place, then he hustled down the hallway just as he saw a nurse swing a rolling chair into the man's belly. He groaned as his breath escaped his lungs and doubled over. Running to the man as he tried getting up, Creed jumped on his back and fought with him to get his arms behind his back. He was punched once in the jaw during the thrashing but heaved out a breath and landed a punch to the man's temple. It hurt his knuckles horribly, but the adrenaline was still thrumming through his body. The man's body went limp and a security guard ran toward them.

Nurses intercepted the security guard and began reciting what happened and a nearby doctor quickly bent down and checked the man's pulse as Creed stood from the ground. He started to walk back to Hope when the guard yelled, "You don't leave."

"I have to get Hope. She's in a room just down the hall. I'll be right back."

The security guard turned at the sound of police running down the hall and Creed took the moment of chaos to get to Hope.

He tried to turn the knob on the door and heard her sob. "Hope, it's me. Creed. Open the door."

"Creed?" Her voice shook.

"Yes, honey, it's me. Open up."

The lock turned and Hope slowly opened the door. Her face appeared in the crack of the door and her eyes landed on his face. She sobbed and threw herself into his arms. He held her close and whispered soft words of comfort. At least that's what he intended. His heart still beat rapidly from his encounter with the assailant, but Hope felt good against his body.

A police officer approached them. "I'm going to need to take your statements."

Hope turned to the police officer. "My legs are shaking so badly; I need to sit."

Creed watched her face as she fought to compose herself and he laid his hand on her shoulder. He could feel her shaking so he remained as he was until she managed to calm.

Addressing the police officer he asked, "Is it alright if you take our statements here?"

14

Hope woke and it was still dark outside. At least, the little stream of light that filtered from the lower right-hand corner of the window around the bottom of the curtain wasn't there. She turned her head to look at the clock on the table between her bed and Grace's. Three a.m.

Chills ran down her body. She sat up and rubbed her arms to warm them.

Her stomach soured as she remembered the night she'd been kidnapped. She'd managed a quick look at her bedside clock—three a.m. She continued to wake up each night around this time. It had screwed up something in her body that seemed to now make this her waking time each day. Maybe she'd see a counselor about changing her body clock, if that would ever be possible.

She twisted and set her feet on the floor. Pushing down the legs of the sweatpants that had crawled up her legs as she slept, she tightened the string at her waist and straightened her T-shirt. Slowly and quietly, she made her way to the door and twisted the knob. Slipping out the door, she carefully pulled it closed and turned to sneak to the bathroom.

She jumped when she saw Creed quietly watching her from the sofa. Her heartbeat raced in her chest, and she held her hand over her mouth to hold her scream back.

"Where are you going?" he whispered.

"To the bathroom."

He nodded, but it was so imperceptible she stared for long moments to make sure she didn't imagine it.

Forcing herself to look away from him, she softly padded toward the bathroom. The only sound was the carpet squishing under her toes and the hum of the air conditioner in the room.

Once she'd made her way to the bathroom, she closed the door and flipped the switch on the wall. The fan switched on with the light, startling her with a sound so loud and obnoxious compared to the quiet of the room a moment ago.

Hope walked to the mirror and looked at herself. Her eyes had dark circles under them. Her hair was a mess. She'd tried putting it into a ponytail before she went to bed. That ponytail now sat at an awkward angle at the crown of her head and the fine hairs around her face had all pulled from the elastic band she'd tied them back with. She actually looked like a mess. A hot mess more like. Behind her dark circles was skin so pale and colorless she didn't even recognize herself. Her cheekbones protruded and her cheeks sank in.

Glancing down at her hands she saw the red marks where the zip ties had bitten into her skin and the bones of her wrists protruded out so stark against her flesh that her stomach twisted. How long would it take to get back to her old self? It felt like never. She didn't even recognize anything about her former self. She'd been strong and so damned sure she was doing the right thing by recording and documenting the congressman. She walked home each night determined to do more tomorrow. Her mind plotted and planned what to do next. Now she could barely think about what lay ahead of her in the next ten minutes. She was afraid of every sound. Every person she saw sent fear running through her body so strongly that it made her weak and feeling as though she'd pass out. Then, the fear of passing out kept her heart beating stronger and harder and there was no way she'd be able to pass out.

She twisted the handles of the water on the sink and moved her hands to feel the water run over them. Closing her eyes, she imagined the fear and ugliness of what she'd just been through washing away from her body. Then she opened her eyes and saw that stark, scared looking woman staring back at her and it all rushed back with such force she thought she'd throw up.

Hope turned off the water, dried her hands on the towel laying alongside the sink and lightly folded it and laid it back down. Taking a deep breath, she turned the knob on the door and froze when Creed stared into her eyes. He was casually leaning against the wall across from the door, but his shoulders were tense. So was his jaw.

"Hi." She whispered.

"Everything alright?"

"Yes."

His head cocked to the right and she felt his disappointment.

"No."

His lips pressed together and lifted slightly to the right, then he held his hand out to her.

She took the three steps toward him and laid her hand in his. He walked her to the sofa and tugged her hand until she sat.

"Tell me what's wrong."

She pulled her hand from his and rubbed her hands up and down her arms. Then crossed them in front of her and willed her heartbeat to slow.

He waited patiently for her and the silence dragged on for longer than she anticipated it would or should. But she was afraid she'd start crying as soon as she told him.

Finally, when it seemed as though he wasn't going to say anything until she did, she shook her head and took a deep breath. "It's three o'clock. That's when I was taken."

She swallowed several times. She wanted to swallow the tears and the fear and that feeling that came over her every damned time she remembered it.

His arm slid around her shoulders and the weight of it felt good. Comforting and right. She relaxed slightly, then leaned over and rested her head against his shoulder and closed her eyes. He made her feel safe and secure and as if everything would be alright. If wishes and dreams could make it come true, she'd wish and dream it over and over again. She wanted everything to be alright once more.

15

Should he touch her? He hesitated so long it felt uncomfortable. She'd been wakened in the middle of the night by strangers who jerked her from her bed and took her to places she didn't know. Always with the threat of being a sex slave or killed. He didn't ever want her to be afraid of him.

When he couldn't take it any longer, he wrapped his arm around her shoulders and held her. His heart beat strong in his chest and he braced himself for her to jump up and run. When she leaned against him and laid her head on his shoulder his body reacted in ways he'd never have guessed. His heartbeat sped up and his stomach felt as though it turned inside. His nostrils flared and the fresh aroma of soap and Hope filled him.

Slowly he leaned them back against the sofa and Hope snuggled closer to him. He closed his eyes and tried memorizing how he felt in this moment. She was slight of build, though now she was very thin and needed to gain back some of the weight she'd lost. But still, his arm fit around her perfectly. Her body's warmth seeped into his body, and he hoped his warmth seeped into hers. She'd acted cold before and he wanted to be her warm. Her comfort. Her safe place. This poor little woman needed that more than anything.

He rested his cheek against the top of her head, and he let out a long breath as he settled further into the back of the sofa. Remembering how she'd looked walking from the bedroom, with his T-shirt and sweatpants on made him feel funny or possessive. She'd likely be a knockout in anything she wore. Dressed for the office or a night out, he could envision what she'd look like. But, wearing his clothes? That played with his mind more than anything else. It was that primal, *me man and I take care of you,* feeling. He'd never felt that way before. It was a little disconcerting.

Soon her soft even breathing reached his ears and he realized she'd fallen asleep in his arms. Tears sprang to his eyes and he swiped them away with his left hand before they fell on her head.

It was stupid to get emotional over this. It was also not like him. At all.

He swallowed and forced his breathing to even out and closed his eyes to simply enjoy this moment. Hope trusted him right now when men had let her down and treated her in the most horrible manner, yet she trusted *him*. It made him feel like he was ten feet tall. He felt powerful with this knowledge and just before he drifted off to sleep he promised to always protect her and never let her down.

∼

A soft clicking woke him and his heart raced at the sound. Hope still lay against him, though the room was beginning to fill with light.

He eased his arm from her shoulders and sat her back gently, then walked to the door of the room, and listened as the security system beeped lightly before the knob turned. He placed his foot against the door to stop it, then glanced out the peephole to see Charly looking up at him.

Taking the doorknob in his hand he pulled it open and stood in front of Charly blocking her way.

"What are you doing here?"

Charly cocked her head to the side and assessed him. "I'm early because I came to bring the girls clothing before they woke up. I thought it would make them happy."

He glanced at his watch and saw that it was five-thirty and shook his head.

Taking a deep breath, he stepped back to let her in. "Sorry. I didn't realize it was that late."

"Rough night?"

"Not really rough. But Hope woke at three this morning. Scared."

Charly shook her head slowly. "Poor thing. It'll take a while I'm afraid."

He nodded then closed and bolted the door. As he stepped into the living room, Hope sat up, her head turned, her eyes stared into his. "Are you okay?"

Hope nodded.

Charly laid a bag on the sofa next to Hope. "I brought you all some clothing. Some of it is new, some purchased from a thrift store. But, all of the clothing is in great shape. The undergarments are all new. Please look through the clothing and help yourself to whatever you want to wear. I think I brought enough for two outfits each."

Hope looked into the bag then sat back up. "I should wait for the others."

Charly smiled at her and sat alongside the bag. "That's very sweet of you, but it'll likely be easier if you just pick what you want now. You can always trade if someone likes what you've chosen. And to be honest, you're all different sizes and I had that in mind when I chose the clothes."

Hope smiled at her but her shoulders shrugged. Charly, not to be daunted, reached in and pulled some clothing from the bag. She stacked the clothing in sets and then the sets were arranged on the coffee table in such a way as they could all be seen.

"I'll be honest with you and tell you when I picked out some of these, I had you in mind. For instance, I thought this would look lovely on you with your dark hair and deep brown eyes."

Charly handed Hope one of the sets of clothing. A rich deep orange and mustard yellow lightweight sweater and a pair of deep orange leggings.

Hope held up the sweater and for the first time in several hours, she smiled. "This is beautiful."

Charly nodded. "I thought so." She leaned forward and held up the leggings. "These have a pocket in them for your phone or money or whatever you want to put in there."

Hope smiled as Charly showed her the pockets on either leg.

Creed watched in fascination as Charly brought Hope out of her despair. He hoped when they left for Washington, she'd perk up and get into helping them take down the congressman and his wife. It had helped all of RAPTOR to get over their anger and frustration with Dildo to go after him.

His phone vibrated and he pulled it from his pocket. A text from Emmy read, "I'm being released today. Therese will be here this morning to take the women home. Should I instruct her to prepare to take you and Hope to Washington DC?"

He nodded his head and looked up at Hope. "We can go to DC this afternoon. Are you sure you want to help us with this?"

16

She swallowed. "Yes."

Creed stared at her for what felt like a long time and her heart began racing at the thought he wouldn't let her go. She needed to put these demons behind her. She needed to finish what she'd started with Congressman Compton and his disgusting wife, Helen Rathburg Compton. They were so dirty and complicit in this trafficking ring, she had to stop them. She was scared, that was a fact, but this time, she had help.

"Okay. I'll let Emmy know." He tapped out the message on his phone and she watched his face. Charly stood with a couple of the sets of clothing and took them in to the room she shared with Grace.

Creed then walked to the kitchen and started a pot of coffee. She watched him move around the kitchen, open the refrigerator, the cupboards then tap his phone screen.

Charly quietly entered the room and took four stacks of clothing into the room where Valerie and Helen still slept.

Hope stood and picked up the orange clothing and the undergarments that Charly had apologetically offered her, not sure of her size, and went into the bathroom to clean up.

Taking a shower felt like a ridiculously wonderful freedom, after not being allowed to shower for sixteen days. She'd never take something so simple for granted. The hotel shampoo smelled fantastic and the sores on her wrist didn't burn this time when the water hit them. Progress.

Hope sighed heavily and ended her shower, knowing the others felt just as she did and wanted to allow them time to enjoy their simple freedoms.

Dressing in her new clothing, the feeling of guilt washed over her as she realized she hadn't even thanked Charly for taking her free time to shop for them. She had to get her head back in the game of life. Enough of her self-pity, it was time to buck up and get shit done.

A soft knock sounded on the door and she jumped, but said, "Yes."

Charly's voice came through the door. "I forgot to give you the brush and comb I'd purchased for you."

Her eyes watered as she unlocked the door. Opening it to see Charly standing before her, her eyes roamed down Hope's body and the broadest smile she'd seen from Charly since she'd met her yesterday lit up her face.

"Everything looks fantastic on you. I should become a personal shopper."

Hope giggled. "You did a great job and thank you so much for putting so much thought and effort and time into helping us."

Hope looked down at her clothing; the warm bright colors made her feel vibrant and they were soft to boot.

Charly held out a small fabric toiletry bag. "I have a brush, comb, some hair ties, a toothbrush, toothpaste, and hand lotion in here for you."

Hope swallowed and inhaled a deep breath. "Thank you, Charly, you're a wonderful person and I am so grateful to you."

Charly laughed again. "I've never been much of a shopper, but Piper has taught me a few things and I'm learning to enjoy the process of walking around a store, touching pretty things, and allowing my mind and body to settle. Plus, we've helped enough women to know that they need the feeling of having something to start with and cleaning up and feeling good again is a great way to begin."

Hope unzipped the side pocket and pulled out a tube of lip gloss in the sheerest shade of copper or coral or some shade slightly orange but not. She'd never been into makeup that much.

"Oh, isn't that the prettiest shade I've ever seen. Thank you so much."

Charly nodded then stepped back as the other girls noticed the clothing in their rooms and chatted loudly about it.

Hope closed the door and quickly brushed her hair. She used the blow dryer, which felt like heaven, then she brushed her hair once more. She brushed her teeth, then decided to try out the lip gloss. The color suited her coloring and went together so well with her outfit that she smiled as she looked in the mirror. She felt pretty once again. Her old self was beginning to emerge.

Gathering her things, she stepped out of the bathroom and saw the other women she'd been held captive with holding clothing and chatting about the colors and how excited they were. Each of them was in their twenties or thirties. She was the oldest at thirty-two. But this scene before her made her both happy and sad. Here they all were acting like they'd never gotten anything new before and that was just sad in a way. What they'd gone through made them all feel as though life would never be good again.

"Are you okay?"

She jumped when Creed spoke to her. She'd been so engrossed in her thoughts she hadn't heard him approach. "Yeah. Mixed emotions I guess."

She looked into his eyes and her breath caught. His lips were full and even stretched into a smile they looked soft. His eyes were dark and shiny, framed with thick full lashes. Light lines at the corners of his eyes added a pinch of maturity and told of a life lived. The beard he wore added to the darkness of his look, but in a way that didn't seem scary to her. The breadth of his shoulders was visible through the T-shirt he wore and the muscles in his upper arms were mesmerizing.

"You look beautiful." His expression was one she'd never seen before.

She swallowed. "Thank you. I was just thinking the same thing about you."

His eyebrows rose and his smile widened. "I've never been called beautiful."

She pursed her lips. "Really? That's too bad."

Then he laughed and she couldn't look away from him.

His phone buzzed and he looked at the screen then winked at her. "Our groceries are here."

He turned to Charly. "I have to go down to the lobby and grab our groceries."

"I'll be here," she responded.

One by one the girls took a shower and dressed in the first set of new clothing they'd had to change into in a while. Creed made breakfast for all of them and she helped him by cutting up peppers and cheese and bacon. He tossed everything together and made the most delicious omelet she'd eaten in a very long time.

He looked at her often and she felt her cheeks warm every time. Despite the fact they were in hiding, it was a wonderful day so far.

"Hope, I have to go for a bit. Charly will be here with you ladies until we leave for the airport. I need to help Emmy get home from the hospital. "

Her heart felt heavy and disappointment weighed her down. Realization that she was a job to him hit her hard and she battled the tears that welled in her eyes.

Nodding, she cleared her throat in an effort to regain her composure. "Of course. I hope Emmy's doing better."

"She is. I'll be back in a little while. You're all in good hands."

17

E mmy settled into the chair in the living room, her laptop on her lap and her mind already at work.

He packed up his belongings and readied to leave for DC. Carrying his duffle out to the living room, he dropped it on the floor next to the door.

Emmy stopped typing. "Creed, tell me what you've learned from Hope."

He told her all Hope had told him and Emmy entered it into their RAPTOR system for the whole team to read.

"I heard back from Roxanne Delany. We can use her home in DC. She said if you need her and Hawk to join you there to help with logistics, she's available."

"Thank you. I'll send them a text."

Emmy smiled and continued typing. "This is what I think we should do. You and Hope head to DC today. Falcon,

Kori, and I will go home to gather some equipment. Therese will drop us off on the way."

Emmy looked at Falcon as he moved into the room and grinned. "Kori and I are getting married while we're at home. Of course, we'd love to have you there with us."

Creed laughed. "Congratulations." He stood and wrapped his friend in a hug then slapped him on the shoulder. "I hate to miss your wedding, Falcon. But I'm so anxious to get to DC and begin laying the groundwork to snag the congressman and his wife. I wouldn't be good being idle. I couldn't even take a nap just now. My nerves are jumping."

"I totally get it, Creed. We'll have plenty of pictures to share with you. My dad and Megan are working hard to get everything ready. We'll be in Washington with you all in a couple of days."

"We'll celebrate then."

Falcon smiled then returned to the kitchen. Creed read over Emmy's notes to see if any changes needed to be made. His mind swirled with everything going on.

Emmy tapped the table. "Okay. Did you see the report Piper just uploaded?"

Creed saw the notification and opened it.

"The Dumonds' phones had been bugged, but we managed to scramble the signals and clear the phones. This may also alert whoever bugged them that someone is on to them. Until we can get to their home and clear it for bugs, we still recommend Hope not tell them where she is and they should be cautious. Creed, when you go to DC, take burner phones with you and give them to the Dumonds. I'd also recommend only texting if you want to talk to them and have them go somewhere out of the house to talk. Not in their cars, we have to clear them for tracking devices and bugs. First order of business when you arrive in DC is to debug the Dumonds' home and vehicles."

Creed nodded. "Okay. I'll stop on my way to the hotel and pick up some phones. I'll take care of their home and vehicles as soon as I get there."

"You may want them to stay at the Bowman home with you and Hope. At least you'll know they aren't bugged and they should be safe there."

Creed swallowed. "I'll offer it up. I assume Roxanne will text me the code to get into the house."

"She will. Also, there's a housekeeper there on a daily basis. Don't scare her. Her name is Carmella. She'll cook and clean and she knows her job, so try to give her some space. If the Dumonds plan to stay at the home, give Carmella a little notice so she can plan."

"Okay. Then I'll get maps of the city and of the congressional office buildings. I'll ask Hope to help me plan a way to get into the building."

"Is that where she hid the recordings?"

"Yes. There and at a store named Byte Me, where she was having copies made. She believes that's how she was found out. So I'll be paying them a visit as well."

"Okay. For the time being, we're going to consider everyone else there at arm's length. No police involvement unless absolutely necessary. Until we know just who's on the congressional payroll as to this operation and how far their reach is, we aren't bringing in any outsiders. I've spoken to Uncle Gaige and if we need additional support, we can bring in GHOST to help us."

Creed nodded and Falcon walked back into the dining area. "Who's coming from RAPTOR?"

"You, Creed, Diego, Donovan, Charly, and Caiden so we have one of our Bravo team members on site if we need them. If we need more support, Hawk will be first from GHOST, and Jax and Dodge have already been there, as well as Wyatt. I'm hoping we don't have to call in GHOST, but it's nice to know they're available if we need them. Mostly, Gaige has contact with Casper, should we need help from the Department of Defense."

18

H ope watched the ladies in the room eat the lunch Charly had delivered. Each of them wore their new outfits and there was a sense of excitement in the room. She felt it in her bones. They were not dirty throwaways, they were people. Women. And there was a new opportunity for life to start over for each of them. Grace, Valerie, and Helen all discussed possibly going to school to learn a new trade. Valerie and Helen decided they'd like to be cops, which was actually a great idea. They could deal with victims from the stance of having been one. Grace mused about becoming an attorney to put away the bastards that Valerie and Helen captured. They laughed about it, but mostly, Hope wanted this for them. The room felt lighter and the women smiled now. The renewed sense of things being normal and promising again felt good.

"Hope. What do you want to do when you get home?" Grace asked.

The question surprised her, though it shouldn't have. They were all sharing their hopes and dreams.

She set her half-eaten chicken tender in the container and sat straighter. "I'm going to bring down the congressman and his wife who had me kidnapped. Then, I'm going to use every ounce of my energy to make sure everyone remembers what pieces of shit they are. And to those people who supported them, I'd like to shame them to the bottom of their being for not digging deeper into the people they elected and gave so much power, only for them to abuse it against the very people who voted for them."

The chatter stopped and four faces stared back at her as if she'd spoken in tongues.

Taking a deep breath, she picked up her half-eaten chicken tender and put it in her mouth.

Grace finally broke the silence. "Well, hell. I didn't see that coming."

Valerie shook her head. "Me either. You've been so quiet and meek; I never expected such vehemence from you."

"Oh, a fire has been lit in my stomach and each day as the drugs wash away, the fire grows. If it kills me in the end, I will do everything I can do to make sure those responsible for so much pain go down and go down hard."

The women, including Charly, sat in silence as they contemplated what she'd said. As the silence wore on, she gathered her thoughts together and told herself to be brave. No matter what happened, someone had to be brave and stop this. Creed and his co-workers were brave.

Look what they'd done to rescue them. She wanted to be like them.

Helen clapped her hands. Then Valerie smiled and she clapped too. Grace and Charly joined in and her cheeks warmed. She inhaled a deep breath, hoping to inhale the bravery she'd just boasted of and their praise for it. She'd need everything she could muster. She'd need it all.

She smiled at them and nodded her head. Then she picked up her disposable soda cup and held it toward the middle of the table. "Here's to all of us taking down those pieces of shit."

The others lifted their cups and they gently tapped, and for the first time in eighteen days she felt pretty fucking good.

Her phone, actually Creed's burner phone, buzzed in her pocket as she helped clean up lunch. She pulled it out and saw his name on the screen. Her cheeks heated and so did the tips of her ears. She was glad he couldn't see her.

"Hello."

"Hi, Hope. It's Creed."

She giggled. "I know."

"Yeah. Okay." He cleared his throat. "So, Emmy says you can call your parents if you like. Their phones were bugged but we fixed that. However, you still can't tell them where you are or that you're coming home. We don't know if their house is bugged. Same with their cars."

"Oh my God. That is so creepy."

"It is. But, let's play this cool. You can ask them to step outside to chat. Keep it short in case their cell signals are also being tracked. We don't know how far-reaching the congressman is. Tell them not to discuss anything in the house or the car and you'll call each day. When we get to Washington later today, the first thing I'm going to do is scan their home and vehicles. Then, you might want to ask them to stay with us so we know they're safe."

She took a deep breath and let it out slowly. "I want them to be safe. Absolutely."

"Well, you and I know we'll be there today. I'll go over first thing, but I can't take you there."

"No, I want to go..."

"Hope. My job is to keep you safe."

Her stomach twisted. She paced the floor. "No, your job is to stop these fuckers."

"That too."

"That first."

"Hope. Listen to me. I can do both."

"If my parents get killed or hurt, it'll kill me. It's all because of me. I can't let anything happen to them."

She heard Creed take a cleansing breath and she pictured him in her mind. She took a deep breath as well and rolled her head on her shoulders. She could see his handsome face, rigid in frustration, his brows slightly pinched, his jaw set. She didn't need to be giving him shit, he was trying so hard to help her.

"We're all working hard on this. We have several team members coming to DC with us. We have equipment and a couple of contacts within the DoD. They may be able to help us, maybe not, but we aren't afraid to ask for everything to ensure that you and your family are safe and that these traffickers are brought to justice."

She sat on the foot of her bed. "Okay."

"If you and your parents feel better, you can ask them to go to a secure, safe hotel for the night and to wait there for us to contact them. Don't mention the name of it. Tell them not to discuss too much until we know what the scope of surveillance is on them."

19

Creed waved the key card in front of the security panel on the hotel room door. The beep sounded, the green light came on and he slowly opened the door to chatter and the smell of freshly popped popcorn.

Stepping further into the room, he tucked the keycard into his wallet and looked around.

Grace saw him first. "Hey, Creed. We're all packed."

Grinning he nodded. "That's great because I just got word the plane has landed. While Therese is filing her flight plans and refueling, we'll load up and drive to the airport. The timing should be perfect."

He glanced across the room at Hope, then he looked at Charly.

Charly grinned from ear to ear. "Yep, they're all ready. We have the two SUV's downstairs. After I drop you all off at the hangar, I'll go back to the house and pick up Emmy, Falcon, and Kori."

"Sounds good. Thanks Charly."

She grinned again then looked at him and Hope, who stared at him. The girls gathered their belongings and waited at the door to leave.

He nodded once then looked at Charly. "Front or back?"

She chuckled, "Front."

Hope's brows furrowed as she glanced between them and Charly laughed. "I'll walk in front of you all, Creed will walk last to make sure we all get out without issues."

He watched Hope's shoulders relax and a sadness fell over him. Charly squeezed between the women and opened the door. Glancing down the hall both ways she then stepped out and nodded for them to follow.

Hope was the last to exit the room, and he noticed her hesitation just before stepping out of the doorway.

"We're here with you. It's alright Hope."

Hope shook her head. "I don't think you can possibly know how it feels to be powerless. To be tied to a wall and told day in and day out how worthless you are. To not have a shower for sixteen days and feel repulsed with your own odor. That's when you believe the things those assholes said to you. That's when you feel dirty, and cheap, and worthless. I won't ever let that happen to me again."

He swallowed the lump that had grown in his throat. It was large and dry and scratchy as it went down. He inhaled through his nose and held for a moment, on the verge of sobbing like a young girl.

"No. I can't imagine." He managed to say. "I'm so sorry you were made to feel that way."

He stayed close as they made their way through the hotel and across the parking lot to their vehicles. The women quickly loaded their belongings and themselves into the vehicles.

He drove the rented SUV with Hope in the passenger seat and Grace in the back seat. Helen and Valerie opted to drive with Charly and he could see them in the rearview mirror. Turning his right signal on, he slowed and turned into the road that led to the hangar. Therese would have the plane ready by now.

From his peripheral vision he could see Hope's fingers twist around each other. She'd finally stopped looking out the side windows to see if they were being followed. Her head twisted back and forth as they drove. He softly said, "It's okay. You're safe." And her cheeks turned pink. She managed to be still for a few minutes, then was compelled to keep a look out for anything out of place.

He located Hangar 49 and honked three times in succession. The doors opened and the RAPTOR plane stood ready to pull out as soon as its passengers were loaded.

From the back seat, Grace gasped. "Wow."

And Hope gawked. "That's so cool."

Hope was quiet. Creed pulled into the hangar and drove to the right and behind where the plane sat, well out of the way of the propellers, turned the vehicle around so they would drive straight out, then waited for Charly to do the same with her SUV.

He nodded once. "Okay, grab your things and we'll go straight to the plane and up those stairs. Inside, stow your things into the overhead bins, find a seat and fasten your seatbelt. This isn't like a commercial plane. Therese will let you know which direction you're heading first."

As the other doors opened he headed around the front of the vehicle to open Hope's door, but she'd already gotten out of the SUV before he could get there. Disappointment flashed then faded as she came to stand alongside him. Grace came to her first and folded her into a hug.

"I'll never forget you, Hope. And I'll pray every day that you find those bastards and bring them down. I'll be watching the news to hear of the congressman."

"We'll be on the plane together Grace."

"I know, but I want to say good-bye now."

Hope hugged her back and they held for a long time. "I'll never forget you either, Grace. I'm going to do the very best I can. I promise you that."

When they pulled apart, Grace stared into Hope's eyes and he saw Hope swallow. Grace smiled brightly. "It's okay to be scared. If you're scared, you'll stay safe. That's what my grandma always said."

"That's good. Because I am."

Grace then turned to him as Helen hugged Hope.

"Thank you so much for saving us Creed. Tell Emmy and Falcon too, please. I hope Kori will be alright and please know I'll never forget any of you."

She hugged him briefly and he hugged her back. Their job meant they didn't always get a thank you, so this was extraordinarily nice.

"I'll never forget you either, Grace. I'll let the others know, and Kori is doing just fine."

The others said much the same, then with smiles on their faces, they boarded the plane to start their lives over once again.

20

He motioned for Hope to sit next to the window on the plane. Falcon and Kori were across the aisle from them and Emmy sat behind. Charly hustled the other women to the back of the plane. The plan was to drop Falcon, Kori, Charly, and Emmy off at Lynyrd Station first, refuel the plane, then immediately leave for Washington. The others would then be flown to their homes.

His stomach felt a bit unsettled. Mostly it was because of the indecision. Hope was likely not in a place in her life to make a big life decision. What she'd just been through was traumatic. The betrayal left a distrust of all others in its wake and only the mentally strong overcame that feeling and learned to trust again. His thoughts had been on her for these past few days. He wanted her. When he wasn't with her, he wanted to be more than anything else. There was absolutely no doubt that he was attracted to her. And she was so different from any other woman he'd ever met. There was definitely a pull to her that he'd never experienced.

He glanced over at her sweet face, now peaceful in sleep. He was glad for that. She hadn't slept well most of the past twenty days or so. A full belly and the feeling of security allowed her that much at least.

"Hey."

He turned to Falcon, who whispered because Kori was also sleeping.

"Yeah."

"When you get to Washington, Hawk and Roxanne will be there. She wanted to check on the house and he thought he could be of use until the rest of us get there."

"That's good. I've been wondering the best plan of action and how we'd get Hope's parents into a vehicle then sit and wait to see if the congressman has someone come to the morgue."

"Yeah. Hawk just texted." Falcon nodded to his phone and Creed pulled his from his pocket and looked at the screen. There it was. He'd been daydreaming and not paying attention. That would get them all in danger, so he needed to put his head on straight and get back in the game.

"Got it."

He tapped the text and read it.

"Roxanne and I will be at the house this evening. The code for you to get in is 5409. It changes weekly. I'll let you know if it changes while you're here."

"Got it. Thank you. Anything we should know?"

"Roxanne and I sleep in her room at the top of the stairs and to the right. It's all gray. The other rooms are up for grabs. Carmella knows you're coming. Stay out of her way. She's been with the family a long time and knows what is required of her. And, if you eat a few meals at the house, you'll need to expand your belt size. Carmella is a top-notch cook. All the comfort foods and generally meat-and-potatoes meals. Enjoy."

"Roger. Thank you. See you tonight."

"Roger."

He turned to Falcon. "When do you plan on getting there?"

"A couple of days. Emmy will come with us."

"And you'll be married."

Falcon grinned then looked over at a sleeping Kori. "Yep."

"It looks good on you."

Falcon grinned again, this time not as big. It was more of a thoughtful grin. "It feels good. Real good. I never dreamed."

Creed nodded. "Yeah. I keep hearing that from the others."

Falcon leaned forward to glance at Hope, then back to him. His left brow rose and Creed shook his head and held both hands up in the air. Before he could say anything, Therese called over the intercom.

"We'll soon be approaching the airport in Lynyrd Station. Please make sure your seatbelts are buckled. We should land in fifteen minutes."

Creed shrugged and buckled his seatbelt, which woke Hope. He smiled at her, "Buckle up. We'll be landing soon."

She looked at her lap then pointed to her still-buckled seatbelt. "Never undid it."

Hope stared out the window as they descended. They were still high in the air, but the outlines of city areas and neighborhoods showed patterns on the ground. The sky was blue, the sun shone brightly. He liked living there and wished he could bring her to the RAPTOR facility for a tour. Maybe after they wrapped up in Washington.

He took a deep breath and let it out slowly then sat back and stared ahead at nothing. From the corner of his eye he saw Falcon kiss Kori and she giggled. It was different for them; they were in a different place. He was happy his friend had found happiness.

Soon they were flying low and Hope turned to him. "It's a small airport."

"Yes. The nearest airport is in Indianapolis which is about an hour drive for us. So, GHOST and RAPTOR helped a local group of pilots raise funds to rebuild this smaller airport. It had been in existence years ago and then abandoned. So the property was there and the hangars were too, though some needed to be rebuilt. Now, it's a functioning airport and we enjoy its use and the proximity to our compounds."

"You all have such power to make change in this world."

Creed thought about that for a minute. "I guess having some money and a larger group of us does help to impact change. It benefits us too."

The plane's landing gear dropped from the body and the hydraulics stopped as they locked into place. Within a minute, they softly touched the pavement, and the engines began to slow. The noise volume increased in the cabin until they came to a stop.

He turned to look at Hope. "Welcome to Lynyrd Station. Though you won't see any of it. This time at least."

"What do you mean by this time? Will I be coming back here?"

He looked into her eyes and realized he was engaging in wishful thinking.

"Maybe. I guess we'll see what happens."

21

They'd refueled quickly and said good-bye to the RAPTOR team. Now, they were near Washington and her stomach tightened. Returning to the city where she'd been kidnapped gave her an unexpected dread. She tried thinking of the good things that would happen here.

Her parents. She'd see her parents.

And, Creed. He was here with her.

After they'd dropped Falcon, Kori, Charly, and Emmy at Lynyrd Station and took off again, Creed held her hand most of the trip. He'd also pulled his laptop out and read reports. Then mid-flight they looked at each other and he kissed her. She liked it. But the other women were still on the plane and that had been it since takeoff.

Creed broke into her thoughts. "So, day after tomorrow, Falcon, Kori, Emmy, Charly, Donovan, Caiden, and Diego will be coming to DC to stay in the house with us. This afternoon, Hawk and Roxanne will be coming in. The house is Roxanne's family home."

"Why didn't they fly here with us?"

"They needed time to gather the intel, pack equipment, and make arrangements for Hank, their baby."

"Okay. Doesn't Therese have to worry about her flight hours?"

"GHOST also has a pilot, Gavin. Between he and Therese, they manage their flight hours and still get us where we need to go."

"Wow. Okay." She braced herself for all that was to come, in more than just the physical. She needed her head on straight. "When can I call my parents?"

"Hawk will go with us to pick up your parents at six o'clock. Piper has called them and made arrangements at Rose Gardens Mortuary."

"Why a mortuary?"

He inhaled deeply and lowered his voice. "We want anyone who is listening or following to believe they are going to identify a body that may be yours."

Her eyes rounded. "What? They'll be so scared."

"They've been told it isn't you, but we want anyone watching or listening to think that you've been killed."

She inhaled a deep breath and let it out slowly. "Is there any chance we can go to my apartment?"

"Why do you need to go there?"

"I have a notebook with names and phone numbers that I think will be instrumental in bringing down everyone involved."

Creed stared at her for a long time and took a deep breath. She loved watching him think.

"I thought you didn't want anything in your apartment."

"I didn't want the recordings in my apartment. The notes, I managed to hide. At least that's what I'd hoped for."

Creed cleared his throat, "Here's what we'll do. Your parents need to call your landlord and tell him they have to close your apartment and move your things out of there. They should do that now. Wait, actually cyber team can do it."

He turned and started typing something into his computer. "What's your landlord's name and the name of your apartment complex?"

"Shayla Jones. And the complex is named Capital City Apartments."

He continued typing, then clicked send.

"Cyber team will call and tell your landlord that you've been kidnapped and are presumed dead at this point. In about an hour, one of them will call your landlord and ask to see an apartment in your building. That will be us. We'll need to disguise you, and Hawk and Roxanne can come with us so we have assistance should something happen."

"Wow. Just like that?"

She laid her hand over her tummy as it rumbled and gurgled and she worried things might be turning sour in there.

"Hey."

She turned to look into his eyes. His brows furrowed slightly and it was the first time she'd seen him look worried.

"It's only a story. Are you close to your landlord?"

"Oh. No." She shook her head. "I know I'm not dead. And, if it's necessary, we can go back one day and explain everything. I'm sure my parents will have to give a sixty-day notice so the apartment will still be there when this is over if I need it. It's just keeping all of this straight."

He leaned forward and kissed her softly on the forehead. "I know this is all foreign to you. I'm sorry if I'm going too fast."

She shook her head. "It's alright. I just have to get out of my own head. Once I'm able to move around a bit I'll be fine. I've just been confined for so long and my thoughts have all been dark and dreary."

"With good reason."

She inhaled and let it out. "Okay." She stretched her shoulders back and sat up straight. "I'm out of my head. Let's make our plans."

He chuckled. "There you go."

He turned back to his computer. "So, when Hawk and Roxanne get into town, we'll all go to your apartment to locate your notebook. Maybe we can sneak some of your clothes out as well. They may very well be watching your apartment, but it'll be light enough that we don't have to turn on lights. And don't be surprised if they've already been in your place looking for any evidence you may have hidden."

She sat straighter. "I've already suspected they'd gone in. I don't think they will have found my notebook though. They'd have to know what they were looking for."

"You mean it isn't a typical notebook."

"Right. It isn't."

"I can't wait to see it."

She grinned but said nothing more.

"After we leave your apartment, we'll go to the mortuary and get your parents. Then we'll wait around to see if anyone comes looking for them. For tonight, it's only Hawk and me so you, Roxanne, and your parents will stay in the SUV."

"Okay."

"Do you know how to shoot a gun?"

"Yes. I'm not super practiced, but when things started getting creepy with the congressman, I joined a women's shooting group. Bought a gun and practiced with them about a dozen times. I can shoot good enough to not hurt myself or anyone else."

"That's good enough."

He sat back and grinned.

"What are you smiling at?"

He turned his head without lifting it off the backrest. "It seems like you're coming back. Not that I really know what you were like before, but your pictures showed a spunky fun-loving woman."

"When did you see my pictures?"

"Babe, cyber has a full file on you."

Her mouth opened then closed then opened again. "What does that mean?"

"It means we compiled a profile."

"Why?"

"Because we needed to know who you are. Who you were. Whether we could trust you."

Her brows furrowed as she let that sink in. "Can I see it?"

"Sure."

He tapped on his computer and a file opened up. She saw her picture on the screen. He lifted his computer and put it on the table in front of her.

"You just tap the up and down arrows to move through the file."

For the remainder of the trip, she scrolled through her file and toward the end, her rage reached an all-time high. How dare they. How dare those sons of bitches do this to her. To add insult to injury, they'd completely trashed her to the world. They said she was a drug addict and wasn't reliable at work. Lies, it was all lies. There would be hell to pay. Hell. To. Pay.

22

Creed ushered Hope from the plane to the large black SUV waiting for them inside the private hangar.

Once they'd both buckled in, he set the GPS and headed for the Bowman home.

After he'd maneuvered the SUV onto the highway, he glanced at Hope. Her anger was still boiling just below the surface.

"You know it's just a smear campaign, right? As soon as we get the dirt on those assholes, we'll clear your name."

"The damage is done. There will always be people out there who will believe I'm a drug addict, troublemaker, and a whore."

He inhaled, "Yes, that's true. But there will also be people who believe Compton was framed, no matter how much evidence we produce. Some people live in their own worlds and want to believe in conspiracies and that they'd never vote for someone so underhanded and dirty."

"My God. Some people are so blind."

"I agree. And yet, we have to live among them. So, you need to decide right now whether you'll rise above it. Despite Compton and company trying to make you look like the bad person here, you know it isn't true. We'll get the evidence on them. We'll bring it to light. We'll expose the dirty horrific things they are doing. Those people who will want to believe the lies spread about you are never going to be your friends or allies. They don't matter."

Her shoulders fell and her head lay back against the head-rest. Creed turned right into the Bowman's neighborhood and was amazed at the posh setting.

"This is incredible."

Hope's eyes scanned the homes on the street, each one its own work of art. "It really is."

She sat forward and enjoyed the homes as they passed by the windows.

The GPS told him to turn right down a narrow street then promptly announced, "You have arrived at your destination."

He drove past the house and turned down a narrow street, then parked alongside a two-car detached garage at the back of a property with an enormous backyard. The stunning home stood tall and proud before him.

"So, this is the back of the house and now I'm not sure if we should walk to the front door or enter from the kitchen. I understand the housekeeper has run of the house and I don't want to scare her."

"Can you text?"

"Let's just go and knock on the back door. If she doesn't answer, I have a code."

As they exited the vehicle, he glanced often at the house. He opened the gate on the white picket fence and held it for Hope. Taking her hand, he walked them toward the back door and relief flooded him when the door opened and a small woman stepped out and waved.

"Miss Roxanne told me to expect you. I'm Carmella."

He smiled at her and waved in return. Once they were only a few steps from each other, he smiled again and nodded. "This is Hope Dumond and I'm Creed Rowan."

"It's nice to meet you Mr. Rowan and Ms. Dumond. Come in."

She hurried inside and Hope followed. He came into the house last, and the aroma of fresh baked bread and a roast wafted to him, wrapped him in a tight hug and made his stomach growl.

Carmella laughed. "Ah, you came hungry. That's good. Ms. Roxanne will be here in an hour, and we'll eat then."

He nodded, "We have a couple of errands to run as soon as she arrives."

"Not until after you all eat. You can't do good work on an empty stomach. Ms. Roxanne needs to keep her strength up. Have you seen the size of her husband? He needs to eat."

Hope laughed and Carmella nodded then turned to the stove, lifted a lid, and stirred the contents before replacing the lid.

"Okay. Come and I'll show you where to sleep."

Carmella led them out the kitchen door and through an area that soon revealed itself to be between a curved staircase alongside the wall to the left. Entering the front doors of this home would be breathtaking. You'd see the sweeping circular staircase to the right, and a set of pillars graced the entrance of a room on either side of the foyer.

Carmella didn't enter into idle chitchat and continued up the staircase. At the top she pointed to a room slightly to the right. "This is Ms. Roxanne and Mr. Hawk's room. You can either sleep at the end of the hall," she pointed to the door at the end of the hall to the left, "where Mr. and Mrs. Bowman slept. Or..." She turned to the opposite end of the hall. "Or you can sleep where Mr. Brendon or Mr. Matthew sleep. They are Ms. Roxanne's brothers."

Creed glanced at Hope then back to Carmella. "Why don't you put us where you think we would be most comfortable."

Carmella shrugged, "Well if Ms. Jax and Mr. Dodge come this time, they sleep in Mr. and Mrs. Bowman's room." She shook her head. "That Ms. Jax is a pistol." Carmella turned to the right and stopped at the first door past Roxanne and Hawk's room. "This is Mr. Brendan's room. You'll be comfortable here. The entire house is comfortable, but this one is large and roomy."

She opened the door and they stepped into a large room with a king-size four-poster bed to the left. There was a sitting area in front of a fireplace across the foot of the bed and beautiful cherry wood dressers on either wall.

Just to the right of the fireplace was a door. "That is your bathroom. You will find all you need inside. Soap, shampoo, conditioner, towels, and washcloths. Everything. I have to go check on my potatoes. Make yourselves at home."

Without any other preamble, she quietly left, closing the door behind her and he smiled at her efficiency and command of the house she clearly loved.

Turning to Hope he watched as she looked around the room, "I think this room is bigger than my entire apartment."

He chuckled, "Mine too."

"She assumed we sleep together."

"She did."

Her cheeks turned an adorable shade of pink and he stepped to her and wrapped her in a hug. "If this makes you uncomfortable, it's clear there are other rooms."

Her head shook before he finished. "No. I just wasn't sure you wanted to sleep with me."

He stepped back and placed his forefinger under her chin. Lifting her face up so he could see her face, he kissed her lips lightly then looked into her eyes. "Not gonna lie, I've thought about it a lot. But I want you to be in the right head space."

23

S he smiled at him. This man was absolutely dreamy.

"I'm not what they said I was. I've never done drugs of any kind. I mean, I've been prescribed pain killers when I broke my arm a few years ago. But I only took two of those. I didn't like the feeling of not being in control." She looked into his eyes for a long time. "When you found me, I was under the influence of drugs, but I didn't take them on my own."

Creed took her hand in his and walked to the foot of the bed. He placed his hands at her waist and lifted her up and sat her on the bed. He took a seat next to her but turned to face her.

"Cowards and criminals resort to smearing someone's good name because they're scared. I'm guessing, and this is a guess, that your parents were asking questions and an investigation into your whereabouts had the congressman deflecting."

She took a deep breath and let it out slowly. "Okay."

"Hey." He turned her face to his. "Get that anger back. Use it. Feel it fully so you can turn it into courage to face that son of a bitch. Because we're going to get him. And you'll have the chance to face him. And you'll need that anger so you can stand tall and show him he didn't succeed in ending you."

Voices sounded from downstairs, and she turned her head.

Creed stood. "I think Hawk and Roxanne are here."

She inhaled a breath so deep her lungs burned, then she let it out slowly and stood from the bed.

"Okay. I just wanted to make sure you didn't believe any of that shit."

"I don't. None of RAPTOR does. And none of GHOST does either."

She nodded her head and he leaned in to kiss her again. She wrapped her arms around his waist and hugged him tightly to her. When their lips parted, she lay her head on his chest. His heartbeat was strong and sure and pure. She soaked up some of his strength; she'd need it over the next few days. And, she'd see her parents in a little while and hopefully all would go well.

His arms circled her body, pulling her close, and she closed her eyes. She liked being in his arms. She liked being in his presence.

Footsteps sounded on the staircase, and he pulled away from her. "Are you ready to meet Hawk and Roxanne?"

"I am."

He kissed her lips once more, then took her hand in his and led her out into the hallway. She turned to the couple just landing on the top step and it took everything she had not to say wow.

Roxanne was a stunningly beautiful woman. Her long white-blonde hair hung to her narrow waist in waves. Her eyes were light blue, her complexion clear. She was simply perfection. Hawk was a stark contrast to his wife. Big—massive actually—with dark hair and dark eyes and muscles on his muscles.

Roxanne smiled and walked toward them. "I'm so happy to meet you. I'm Roxanne." She looked to her husband and smiled. "This is Hawk."

When she managed to find her voice, it came out as almost a squeak. "Hi. I'm happy to meet you. Both. Happy to meet you both."

Hawk grinned and nodded then he and Creed embraced, as men do, with a slap on the back and a gruff squeeze. "Happy to see you again Creed. You've been on the road for a while now."

"I have. Good to see you."

Creed leaned in and kissed Roxanne's cheek and gently hugged her. Nothing like he'd just hugged Hawk. "You look gorgeous as always."

"Thank you. You look well and happy."

Creed nodded and stepped back to stand next to her.

Roxanne looked at her, "I hope you'll be comfortable here. This house used to be filled with three kids running around and my parents trying to keep control. Now, my parents are gone and we're all grown up. Poor Carmella keeps the house for us but complains about how lonely it is here these days."

"Your home is lovely. And I'm sorry about your parents."

Roxanne shook her head. "Thank you. It was hard, but it brought Hawk to me and that has been wonderful."

Hawk smiled at his wife and Hope could only stare. "How did you two meet?"

Roxanne spoke first. "Hawk and Wyatt broke into this house."

"We didn't break in."

"You did too. You broke in."

"We were on a mission."

"To break in here."

"Jesus, this never ends." Hawk rolled his eyes and turned his attention to Creed. "Do you have a few minutes to talk about what we're going to do tonight?"

Roxanne laughed. "Coward."

Hawk leaned down and picked up a suitcase and carried it to the bedroom next to theirs. When he returned he motioned to Creed. "We can chat in the office."

The two men made a quick escape down the stairs and Roxanne giggled. "Do you mind if we visit while I unpack?"

"Not at all."

Hope followed her into the bedroom. It was large, but not as large as the one she and Creed were in. And decorated beautifully in hues of gray and silver.

Roxanne opened her suitcase and began transferring the clothing into the dresser. "Please take a seat and make yourself comfortable. I won't be long. I've only brought a few things and we're only planning on being here for a couple of nights. Sophie is taking care of Henry, our son. I don't like leaving him for too long."

"How old is he?"

Her smile was breathtaking, "He's twenty months old."

"Wow. Is he a good baby?"

Roxanne stopped unpacking and turned to look at her, a serene smile on her face. "He's just the best baby ever."

Creed knocked on the door frame and looked in, his eyes landing on hers. "Carmella says we have to eat before we go, so..."

Hope stood and walked to Creed; Roxanne chuckled behind her. "Carmella is in a mood because we didn't bring Henry. She'll be fine."

Creed grinned, "That explains the mood change."

24

Creed pulled into the parking lot of Capital City Apartments. Both he and Hawk were scanning the area. He glanced in the mirror and saw Hope doing the same thing. She had her hair piled high on her head and two pencils tucked into it to hold her knot in place.

He backed into a parking spot directly in front of the door and Hawk jumped out, opened the back passenger door and helped Roxanne from the vehicle. He watched in the mirror as they walked into the manager's office.

Creed then looked at Hope in the mirror and grinned. "You look like the prettiest nerd I've ever seen.

She smiled. "Flattery. You jocks are all alike."

He laughed at her sass, mostly because he wasn't expecting it. Her smile and the pink in her cheeks added to her cuteness.

He caught the manager's door opening and he said, "It's go time. Are you ready?"

She inhaled and let it out in a loud whoosh. "Yep."

Creed stepped out of the vehicle and opened Hope's door. She stepped out, looking absolutely adorable in her jeans, which were Roxanne's and much too long, rolled up, and her tennis shoes with no socks. Totally geeky.

He took her hand and they followed Hawk and Roxanne into the main building. The manager turned to look at them and Hawk said, "This is my brother and his girl-friend. They're helping us find the perfect place."

As the manager, Shayla, looked at Creed and then Hope they all waited to see if there would be recognition. There was none, and when Shayla nodded and continued down a hallway, Hope let out the breath she was holding and he squeezed her hand.

"So, this apartment still has the tenant's items in it, but her parents have asked us to try and rent it out. They'll be moving her things out soon."

Shayla unlocked the door and they stepped inside.

He felt Hope stiffen as they stepped into the apartment, and it had indeed been ransacked. The cushions had been pulled from the sofa and chairs, the drawers in the kitchen had been removed and dumped, the small desk by the window in the living room had its drawers dumped and they laid on the floor amid the rubble.

Shelves on the wall had all been cleared and all contents on the floor.

Shayla gasped. "Oh my God. What in the hell..."

Hawk spoke quickly, "This place looks as though it's been tossed. What happened to the tenant?"

"I'm told she was kidnapped and is presumed dead."

Roxanne looked around, then softly said, "Someone was looking for something."

"I'm sorry folks, I wouldn't have shown you this apartment if I'd known the condition it was in."

Hawk shrugged, "It's alright. It isn't your fault. If we're careful can we step through to see the rooms?"

Shayla looked unsure then Creed stepped further into the room. "We'll be quick, we just want to see the size of the bedroom and the bathroom."

"Um, sure." Shayla responded, then her cell phone rang, and she looked at Hawk.

"Go ahead, we won't be long."

Shayla stepped into the hall, leaving the door open, and he tugged Hope's hand. "What room do you need to get into?" he whispered.

She swallowed a few times then squared her shoulders. "The bathroom." She nodded toward the hallway.

He led her to the bathroom, and she stepped inside to see much the same condition of items strewn around the floor.

Hope stepped in and softly said, "I need my tampon box."

He rotated his head on his shoulders then hesitated. Hope stopped and looked at him. "I need help finding it."

"I'm not...I don't..."

He wasn't squeamish about much, but feminine products, he drew the line there. Plus, it seemed just too personal now.

Roxanne nudged him away from the door. "I'll help. Seriously you guys, they're just tampon."

Hope dropped to her knees and started pushing things around to find her tampon box and he and Hawk stood in the hallway to block Shayla should she come back in.

Roxanne held up a box, "Here it is."

Hope took the box from Roxanne and started pulling tampons from the box. "I have two wrappers taped closed. I need to find those."

Roxanne started looking at each tampon and Hope held one up. "Here's one of them." She pointed to the tape and Roxanne began looking through the others in the box. "Here it is."

Hope took it from her and tucked the tampons into the front pocket of her jeans as she and Roxanne stood. They walked out of the bathroom as Shayla walked back into the apartment.

"I'm sorry about that. What do you think about the apartment, besides its need to be cleaned?"

Hawk nodded. "It could work for us. Do you have any others we can see?"

"I don't. We don't have vacancies very often, that's why I needed to show you this one."

They walked out of the apartment and Creed stepped close to Hope and took her hand. It was cold and shaking, but she'd been a trouper and hadn't crumbled when the door to the apartment opened. He squeezed her hand for reassurance and turned back to Hawk. "We'll wait for you in the SUV."

Hawk nodded and finished speaking with Shayla while he ushered Hope to the SUV. He opened the back driver's side door and she slid in. He closed the door and jumped in the driver's seat. He could hear the wrappers crinkling as Hope pulled them from her pocket.

The back passenger door opened and Roxanne jumped in next to Hope. Hawk soon joined him in the front. He and Hawk turned to see Hope opening the tampon wrappers and pushing the plastic plunger up to remove note pages carefully so they didn't rip. Her hands were still shaking as she unfolded the tightly wound papers and after she'd pried them open and looked at them she burst into tears.

25

———

They were there. All of them. She handed them forward to Creed who opened them and read them, then handed them to Hawk who was snapping pictures of each page.

"Great work, Hope."

She sniffed and swiped at the tears. She was so afraid all that she'd gone through would be for nothing. She was so relieved when she saw the papers still where she'd hidden them that she burst into tears.

"I can't..." She swallowed, swiped the moisture from her face and tried again. "I can't believe it. I was so afraid. I was so nervous. They're here."

Roxanne opened her purse and handed her a tissue and Hope smiled at her, at least she hoped it was a smile because she was still shivering and her mouth felt like it was twisted into a half-crying half-nervous mask of horror.

"Thanks."

She blew her nose and sniffed and Roxanne handed her another tissue which she used to dry her eyes.

She took a deep breath and let it out slowly. "How do you all do that all the time?"

Roxanne giggled, "For the record, I don't."

Hope laughed then and it felt good. Fantastic. It felt fantastic.

She looked up at Creed who still peered around the seat and smiled. "I didn't break down. Those fuckers trashed my place and I didn't break down."

His smile was brilliant. "I'm so proud of you Hope. You were a rock star."

"So were you." She glanced at Hawk. "Thank you. You could have been an actor." Then she turned to Roxanne. "You too Roxanne, wow."

Hawk laughed and Creed smiled at her. She leaned forward and kissed his lips. "Thank you."

His smile was priceless. "Anytime. Now, buckle up, we've got another job to do."

"My parents!"

He nodded, turned toward the front and started the SUV. The others fastened their seatbelts, and she followed suit. Creed pulled from the parking space and eased them from the parking lot and out onto the road. He glanced at Hawk. "You want to text Emmy and tell her we were successful at Hope's apartment, and you'll be uploading photos soon, and that we're on our way to pick up her parents?"

"You got it."

Hawk stopped taking pictures of the little notes Hope had saved and texted out a message. She took a deep breath and tried to get her hands to stop shaking. Roxanne leaned over and placed her left hand over Hope's right hand and squeezed. She whispered, "You did good, Hope."

Hope stared into Roxanne's light blue eyes and only nodded. She'd start crying again if she tried to say anything. Her bottom lip quivered again and Roxanne smiled at her. Then she pulled her hand away and looked out the window.

Hope watched the scenery flow past them as they drove toward the Rose Garden's Mortuary and looked forward to seeing her parents once again. Anytime a thought crept into her mind that the congressman could have someone there to make sure she was dead, she forced it out of her mind and focused on hugging her mom and dad. Oh, that was going to feel so good.

Creed slowed the vehicle down and turned on his left signal. She looked in the direction they were turning and she saw the building. Rose Garden's Mortuary was a pretty place on the outskirts of DC in a suburb named Silver Acres. The landscaping was lush, the flowers were in bloom and gorgeous and the trees full grown and stately. You wouldn't know the place held dead bodies and so much grief.

Creed pulled into the parking lot along with three other vehicles.

"Hope, are any of these vehicles your parents'?"

Her shoulders fell, "No."

"It's alright, we're a little early."

She swallowed. "Okay."

He parked at the end of the parking lot by backing into a spot. Turning the ignition off he unbuckled his seatbelt and glanced at Hawk.

"Think we wait here or go inside to see if anyone has inquired about Hope?"

"I think you stay here and I'll go inside." Hawk responded.

"I have comm units in my duffle in the back."

Roxanne turned to grab the duffle from the back. She pulled it up to her then twisted and handed it to Hawk. He unzipped it and pulled two boxes from inside. "Here you go. I'll let you know what's going on inside. But, first, I'm going to walk around the back, just in case."

"Roger." Creed opened the small box and pulled an earpiece from it and tucked it into his ear. The separate control box that operated it was turned on and the green light showed it was ready. Hawk did the same and glanced back at Roxanne before opening his door.

"Love you, Luna."

She smiled. "I love you right back."

He glanced at her briefly and nodded, then opened his door and walked to the back of the building on the sidewalk. As soon as he was out of sight she heard his voice through Creed's earpiece.

"Clear back here. No cars, only a dumpster. There's a garage, though; I'll check it out."

"Roger." Her heart raced as she waited, though she thought Roxanne was likely more nervous that she was right now.

"Why did he call you Luna?"

"It's a nickname my grandfather gave me. Hawk liked it and picked it up."

Glancing at the gorgeous, composed woman next to her she noticed her jaw was tense and her posture stiff. Reaching forward, she lay her right hand over Roxanne's left and squeezed. Roxanne's eyes landed on hers and a soft smile adorned her lips.

"A van in the garage with Rose Garden's Mortuary written on the side."

"Roger."

A car pulled in and Hope stretched her back to see through the side window. "That's them."

She swallowed the sob that almost flew from her mouth, then slapped her hand over her lips.

Creed looked back at her. "Stay in here. Do not come out for any reason."

She nodded.

"Say it, Hope."

She managed to keep the sarcasm from her voice. "I'll stay here."

Creed stepped from the SUV and walked toward her parents' car. Another car slowly passed by, then continued on its way, and Roxanne sat up straighter to watch.

Creed's steps picked up as he approached her parents' vehicle and he crouched down on this side of the car, where he couldn't be seen from the road. Hope tried looking through the windows of the other vehicles to see what was going on but it was impossible to see.

The car that had slowed down on the road came back and turned into the lot. Hope almost lost her lunch.

26

Creed peered over the side of the car through the windows.

"Stay right where you are. Don't get out of the car."

Hope's parents nodded and Creed shuffled along the ground to the front of the car before the car that had just entered the parking lot passed.

"Hawk, the black Cadillac that slowed came back and turned into the lot."

"I'm on my way back. Where are you?"

"I'm crouching on the ground at the front of the Dumonds' car. Black Buick."

"Roger. Coming along the north side of the building now."

Creed watched the Caddy slow behind Hope's parents' car. Slowly, he pulled his gun from its holster at his side and readied for action.

The Caddy continued on to a parking space two cars over and parked.

"Hawk, the Caddy parked two cars over."

"I have visual. Did they see the Dumonds in the car?"

"Affirmative."

"Fuck. They're under surveillance."

"Agreed. I'm going to tell them to go inside. Go back around and enter the building through the back door and bring the Dumonds to the back door and out to our vehicle."

"Roger. Going in now."

Peeking over the hood of the Dumonds' car, he watched the shrubs move as Hawk moved. He squat walked to the driver's door and motioned for Mr. Dumond to roll his window down. He holstered his gun, then pulled his phone from his pocket and tapped out a message as the window was coming down. Creed looked up at him and held his forefinger to his lips. He then turned his phone around so Mr. Dumond could read the screen.

"Go inside. My partner, Hawk, is waiting for you and will bring you around through the back door. Leave your keys, I'll bring your car to our location."

Mr. Dumond read the screen then looked into his eyes. He saw Hope's eyes starting at him. Brown eyes the shape of almonds, though hers were prettier. When Mr. Dumond made no effort to move, he swiped the screen on his phone and pulled up his ID with his photo. He should certainly know the name by now thanks to Piper.

Mr. Dumond looked at his phone screen then to him once more. Mr. Dumond inhaled deeply, then looked over at his wife. "Shall we go and get this over with?"

She swallowed, then nodded and opened her door. Mr. Dumond pulled the keys from the ignition and handed them to Creed before opening his door.

Creed crept back to allow the door to swing open, then slowly stood as the Dumond's walked with each other, hand in hand, to the front door of the mortuary.

"Hawk, they're on their way in."

"Roger. I'm here in the front of the building to greet them."

Creed heard the door close and looked over to see two men walking away from the Caddy.

"Caddy guests are following. Two."

"Roger."

Creed stepped away from the Dumonds' car and acted as if he'd just exited the vehicle next to them. One of the men from the Caddy turned to watch him, the other continued to walk forward. Creed proceeded to walk behind the two men.

In his ear he heard Hawk. "I'm Hawk with GHOST...uh, RAPTOR, please follow me quickly."

He heard Hawk's breathing increase and he whispered, "At the door."

One of the men turned to Creed and narrowed his eyes. The bald man was obvious in his actions. He wore a black suit, which could look as though he were in mourning, but he allowed the jacket to remain unbuttoned and his gun showed when a gust of wind caught it. The other wore dark dress slacks and a dark blue button-up shirt. He wore his gun in a holster inside his waistband, the butt of his pistol rose above his waistband.

As they reached the door, the bald man turned to him once more and nodded. Creed nodded in return as he heard Hawk in his ear.

"Outside. Heading to the SUV."

The bald man looked at his ear, then out the door. He apparently didn't see anything and Creed maintained his steely stare at the man, who seemed reluctant to turn around.

A clerk from behind the glass window at the mortuary addressed the second man. "Hello. How may I help you today?"

The man's voice was almost robotic when he responded. "We're here to see the body of Hope Dumond."

"Hope Dumond?" The clerk looked at the computer screen. Her brows furrowed as her fingers clicked with her mouse. The bald man continued to turn and look into his eyes, Creed continued to assess him with disgust.

"In the SUV."

The bald man looked at his ear again and Creed shrugged a shoulder. The bald man looked out the window as the SUV slowly left the parking lot. Creed turned and walked out the front door. He hurried to the Dumonds' vehicle and jumped in. Wasting no time in starting the car he quickly backed from his parking spot and took off as the two men exited the building.

They made no move to shoot at him. "Hawk, they aren't shooting."

"Roger. I'll pull off up here and we'll scan for tracking then disable it until we can remove it."

"Roger."

Creed followed the SUV, he could see Hope looking back often, then hugging her mother close. His breathing remained steady, his eyes shifted between his mirror and the SUV. He could see the Caddy behind, though it was a distance behind.

"Hawk, they're too close to stop for long."

He heard Hawk, "Roxanne, honey look in the duffle for the tracking disabler."

Hawk then replied to him. "Creed, slow down and let the Caddy catch up. Once they're close, make the left at Sumptner Road without a signal. Do it quick to see if you can shake them. It'll only be for a couple of minutes, but it'll give us a bit of time."

"Roger."

He slowed his vehicle and saw the Caddy pass a couple of cars on the left to catch up to him. He continued his pace until he saw the Caddy once again pass a car on his left. Timing couldn't have been more perfect, as Sumptner Road was right there.

Creed turned the wheel on the Dumonds' Buick; the tires screeched at the abrupt maneuver. He glanced to his left to see the Caddy speed past, unable to get over because of the car on its right.

"Hawk, I've lost them."

"Perfect. Up ahead on the left is a driveway covered in trees. Back in. I'm already out of the SUV and waiting."

Creed drove up the road, saw Hawk standing at the end of a driveway. He was impossible to miss. He passed just enough to back into the driveway, and Hawk was already scanning under the car with the disabler. Just as Creed opened the door, Hawk's disabler beeped and Hawk pushed the button which would scramble the signal on the tracker. As soon as that was complete, he opened the back door and held the disabler into the car to disable the bug inside. Another loud beep and Hawk grinned.

"See you at home bro."

27

Hope's stomach knotted up tighter than an iron fist. Her breathing came in short spurts and her mother, bless her heart, remained quiet by her side, holding her hand far too tight, but then again, not tight enough. They'd barely had time to hug and Hawk had asked for quiet so he could hear Creed.

Her father sat in the passenger seat in front and glanced back at her often. So often, Hope saw the tears in his eyes. That made tears flow in her eyes. It also made her mother cry. Roxanne sat stoically on the other side of her mother, her eyes blinking furiously.

She swiped her eyes with her left hand, her mother wouldn't let her right hand go for anything. A nuclear bomb could hit them right now and she'd go out with her mother gripping tightly to her hand. She tried watching through the back window as Creed navigated the roads here in DC, which were a pain on the best day, but he drove her parents' car just like he'd drive his own. Wait, probably not. Better than his own. Chances were good, in the line of work he did, his own vehicle saw its share of swerving, speeding, dodging, and ducking on any given day.

She tried listening for anything Creed had to say, but right now they were quiet, focused, and wary.

She turned to see if she could see the Caddy that had been in the parking lot at the mortuary. She'd watched that car like a hawk as it sat in the parking lot and she watched first her parents, then those men, walk into the mortuary. The car was nice, but there were no personal tchotchkes in it at all. Nothing hanging from the mirror. No stickers. Nothing. Probably because those assholes were hit men. Or something. They weren't honest. They weren't honorable. They...

"I remember the license plate of the Cadillac."

Hawk looked into the mirror at her. "Write it down."

She glanced around as if paper and a pen would magically appear, then Hawk said, "Use your phone. Roxanne, help her please."

She saw Roxanne pull her phone up from where it lay in her lap and open a notes app. "Go ahead, Hope."

"JE 8729."

"Got it."

Hawk glanced at Roxanne in his mirror. "Text Emmy, honey."

Roxanne typed out her text and Hope winced as her mom squeezed her hand too tight.

"I'm sorry, honey."

"It's okay, Mom."

"You've lost too much weight."

She kissed her mom's cheek. "We'll talk once we get to the house."

Her mom sniffed and Hope kissed her cheek once more and laid her head against her mom's. Her dad turned once again and smiled then turned forward and wiped the side of his face with his hands. Those fuckers had really messed with her parents and for that, she'd make them pay. Whatever she had to do. Creed was right, get mad. Use it. She was going to and that was a fact.

Creed turned left into the neighborhood where Roxanne's home was located and she whispered to her mom, "We're almost there."

"Where are we staying?"

Hope pointed to Roxanne with their clasped hands, "At Roxanne's family home. Wait till you see it. It's spectacular."

Roxanne winked and her mood lifted slightly. Just being in the neighborhood and knowing they'd soon get out of the vehicle felt like a relief.

Creed turned again and then again and Roxanne said, "Hawk, pull into the garage. I brought the opener. There should be room for the Dumonds' car as well."

His grin was large. "You're the best, Luna. Creed did you hear that?"

"Roger. Pull into the garage."

They navigated down the back street where the garage was located and Roxanne tapped the garage door opener she'd pulled from her handbag. The door silently slid open, and Creed pulled in on the left side. Hawk deftly parked the SUV on the right. As soon as the vehicles had shut off, Roxanne closed the door and they opened their doors and stepped out.

As soon as her mom had stepped from the SUV, she pulled Hope into a big bear hug. It felt amazing. No, better than amazing. Fantastic. No, better than that. It felt like everything. She'd missed this so much.

Soon her father was beside her. "I get a hug too." Her mom released her and immediately she was wrapped in her father's warm strong arms. She sobbed into his chest and released all she needed to release. They'd been so scared. Worried. Her father had lost weight and his face was more lined than it had been when she last saw him. Her mom too. Commotion around them had them pulling away to see Creed, Hawk, and Roxanne grabbing the bags they'd packed from the car and her father stepped to Roxanne. "I can take that honey. You shouldn't carry our stuff."

Hawk smiled and nodded at her father, then wrapped his big beefy arm around Roxanne's shoulders and led them out the single door to the backyard of the Bowman home.

Her mom walked on one side, her father on the other and she looked around for Creed. He walked alongside her father and winked at her when their eyes met. Yeah, he was wonderful. She'd thank him later.

Inside the home, Carmella had more food cooking and the house smelled wonderful. She bustled around the kitchen pulling glasses and plates from the cupboards. "I have roast chicken. It'll be ready soon."

Roxanne giggled. "Carmella, we're alright, please don't worry."

"I worry, Miss Roxanne. Mr. Hawk is a big man, and he needs to eat."

Hawk laughed and leaned in and kissed Carmella's cheek and she simpered. Roxanne laughed and turned to face her parents.

"Welcome to my childhood home, which is your home for as long as you need it. This is Carmella, she's been with our family since before I was born. Her food will fatten you and you'll want for nothing."

Her father reached forward and shook Roxanne's hand. "Thank you for your hospitality. We appreciate all you've done and are doing."

"It's my pleasure. Now, how about I show you to your room?"

"I can do it Miss Roxanne."

"It's alright Carmella. I can manage and I need to freshen up anyway."

Roxanne looked at her parents and smiled. "Please follow me."

Hope went along with them but glanced back to see Creed talking to Hawk. He did glance her way and smile though, and that made her heart beat a bit faster. As they walked up the grand staircase, Roxanne told them about the history of the house and her family, and as Roxanne walked past the door to her room with Creed, her heart went into overdrive. "This is where Creed and Hope are, and you two will be right next door to them here."

Both of her parents turned to look at her and her face felt like it was on fire. "We have a few things to talk about."

28

Creed sat at the dining room table with his laptop open, his report to RAPTOR almost finished. Hawk walked in and sat at a forty-five-degree angle to him at the head of the table with his laptop.

"Any report back on the license plates?"

"Not yet."

Hawk opened the lid on his laptop and started typing something. "I'm uploading the photos of the notes Hope had hidden."

"Fantastic."

Roxanne entered the room. "You know you two can use the office if you like."

"It's too formal in there." Hawk replied.

Roxanne laughed. "I suppose we could do some remodeling. Change things up so more than two people can have space to work in there."

Hawk looked up at his wife, who now stood next to him with her hand on his shoulder. "You could save money and put eight-foot tables end to end and a bunch of us could sit in there."

"Mr. Hawk, you can't do that."

Hawk laughed as Carmella stood looking horrified at the suggestion.

Roxanne laughed too. "Don't worry Carmella. Any work in there will be designed by someone without eight-foot table taste."

"Thank goodness." Carmella continued entering the room with the pitcher of tea and glasses she carried. Setting it on the table she looked at Hawk. "No offense Mr. Hawk."

He grinned at her. "None taken Carmella."

She nodded and left the room. Roxanne began pouring glasses of tea when Hope and her parents entered the room. Roxanne smiled, "Would you like iced tea?"

Hope nodded, "I'd love one please." She turned to her parents. "Mom? Dad?"

Hope pulled the chair out next to Roxanne for her mother. "Please sit and we can fill you in on things."

Her mom sat, her dad next to her mom, and Hope walked around the table and sat next to Creed and across from her parents.

"First of all, I'd like to formally introduce you all. My father, Kole Dumond and my mother Carolyne Dumond. Mom and Dad, this is Roxanne Delany." She smiled at Roxanne. "Her husband Hawk Delany." Then Hope looked at him and smiled. "And this is Creed Rowan."

Hellos were exchanged then Hope continued. "You already know that Creed works for RAPTOR. He works with Piper, who you've spoken to on the phone. There are..." She looked at him and he grinned.

"Nine of us."

"Yes. Nine. But Hawk works for a sister agency, GHOST."

Her father and mother looked down the table to Hawk and then at Creed once again. He got this uncomfortable feeling as her father stared at him, which seemed off, but he took a deep breath, squared his shoulders and closed the lid on his laptop.

Hope continued. "Creed and his co-workers, Falcon and Emmy and Falcon's girlfriend..."

He interrupted, "His wife by now."

"Oh, really? That's so cool." Hope smiled then turned to her parents, but then stopped and looked at him. "But you missed their wedding."

"I did, but we needed to be here, and you need to be safe."

"But..."

He chuckled. "It's all good. The other team members will send me pictures and I'll call Falcon later and congratulate him. It happens. He understands."

Hope's shoulders dropped. "I'm sorry."

Creed turned toward her and laid his hand along the side of her head. "Really, it's okay."

Her eyes stared into his for a long time before she finally nodded.

She turned back to her parents. "So, Creed, Falcon, Kori, and their boss, Emmy rescued me and three other women from a boat in Florida. We were just out of US jurisdiction. The other three women were kidnapped in various locations and stolen to be trafficked."

Her mother gasped and her father began to fidget in his seat.

"I was taken from my apartment in the middle of the night."

"Oh my God." Carolyne mumbled.

"Congressman Compton had me kidnapped."

Kole looked at his daughter, his jaw was tight. "Why on earth would he do that?"

"Because I'd been gathering information on him. He's involved in a huge trafficking ring. He makes millions of dollars a year on trafficking women and children. I pieced it together from phone calls, dates, deadlines, and emails I'd found. I kept a list of names and phone numbers of the people I believe to be involved with him. Those two men today at the mortuary were likely there to make sure it was my body on a slab in there. Compton doesn't want me to be able to give any evidence against him and his wife, who is also involved."

Her parents were quiet for a long time. Her mother began crying and her father wrapped his arm around her shoulders and pulled her close.

"It's so wrong." Her mother sobbed.

Roxanne stood and exited the room. She returned shortly with a box of tissues and gently set them in front of Carolyne before sitting back down.

Carolyne took a tissue and dabbed at her eyes and nose. She looked up at Hope, "Did they hurt you?"

Hope took a deep breath. "They tied me up." She held up her hands to show her parents the scabs and bruising on her wrists. "They didn't feed me much; a couple of meal bars a day. And, Mama, they didn't rape me."

Carolyne sobbed once again, "I'm so happy for that. I was so worried what was happening to you. Then those rumors came out that you were on drugs and often didn't show up for work. We knew that wasn't you, but even the news reported it. Congressman Compton said as much on the news."

"He lied." Hope hit her fist on the tabletop.

Creed wrapped his arm around Hope's shoulders, and she slightly relaxed into him. "It's alright. We'll get it retracted and we'll make sure everyone knows the congressman is dirty."

"His wife too. They're both in on it."

Kole cleared his throat. Creed guessed his age at around late forties, maybe early fifties. Hope took after him most. Same dark hair, same dark eyes. Though she needed to gain some weight back, she was slight of build and her father wasn't at all a large-boned man. He was tall and thin but in good shape. Carolyne was shorter, about the same height as Hope, and was medium boned in stature. They made an attractive couple.

"How did you find out what the congressman was doing?"

Hope swallowed and lay her hands on the table.

"I was working at the office and a call came in from Anton Smith. I recalled seeing his name mentioned recently in regard to the whole blowup in Las Vegas with the Sinners and that whole mess. Anton owns SmithCo, a large media conglomerate. Television, news, newspapers, and he managed to keep most of it out of the media. But I also watch a few cable news channels and am able to get other news that way. So, when he called, I paid attention because I knew he was in hiding. So, I listened."

"Oh, Hope." Carolyne whispered.

"Mom, doing the right thing isn't easy. I had no idea it would go like this, but I knew something was going on that wasn't right. And, I wanted to know what Compton knew or was involved in. I was working for him. If he was doing illegal stuff, I wanted nothing to do with it."

"But you could have been killed."

ope nodded, "I could have been. I thought I was going to be killed. If it hadn't been for Creed." She turned and looked at him, her smile soft but sweet. "I may have been. You should have seen them. We were being held, tied to hooks on the wall of the boat, and Falcon came down first and untied Grace. Then Creed came down and untied Valerie, Helen, and I and helped us out of the lower cabin. We had to be quiet because one of the guards slept in the cabin next to us. Just as we made it up on the deck of the boat Falcon and Creed had to fight to keep the guards from killing us all. Kori was shot in the shoulder in the process. But we made it. We made it."

She took a deep breath and let her breathing slow. "They got us on a smaller boat and took us to Miami where we were taken to the hospital to be checked out. I had been drugged a lot and had to be flushed. But, Creed was there the whole time. Or most of it, actually."

She looked into his eyes and he smiled at her and nodded.

"And now you're sharing a room?" Kole added.

"Yes. We're together." She fibbed. But she didn't want it to be a fib. Now more than ever, she didn't want it to be a fib.

"Don't you think it's because he rescued you?"

"I've given that some thought. It could be. It might be. But I don't think so."

"But, it's so soon after..."

Hope held up her hand. "Dad, after all I've been through, can't I be happy? Maybe it won't last, but we can't know that."

Carolyne looked at her husband. "Let it be Kole. This isn't the time."

Her father shook his head. "I'm sorry. Of course you have the right to be happy." He looked at Creed then, "I'm sorry, Creed. I didn't mean to be disrespectful. I'm...we're so grateful for what you and your teammates did to save Hope and the others."

Creed smiled at her parents. "No disrespect taken. Please know that Hope and I both know this could be fleeting. We're adults and she's been through so much. We're taking it slow. One day at a time."

Her dad nodded then looked across the table. He reached his hand out and she laid her hand in his and squeezed.

Her mom lightly cleared her throat. "So, what happens now?"

Creed laid his forearms on the table. "Hawk and I were just communicating with headquarters. We sent the license plate number from the Cadillac that followed you today. RAPTOR is running it. Before we went to the mortuary, we went to Hope's apartment, and she had notes hidden in there with names and phone numbers. Hawk was just uploading those to our systems. We have a top-notch cyber team, and they'll do the cyber investigation. They'll pull profiles on the names Hope had. They'll find out who owns the Cadillac, and we'll get an address. We also have an electronics store to check out. After that, my teammates will begin arriving day after tomorrow and we'll then make plans to get into the congressional building where Hope has stashed more notes."

"That sounds dangerous."

"It is."

Hawk nodded. "It's what we do. We're trained. We have the manpower, knowledge, and expertise to do what we do."

Her father assessed both men and Hope watched him process all of the information he'd been given. "Should we go stay somewhere else? If you have teammates coming in, it'll be crowded here."

Hawk laughed. It was genuine and rich. "You've seen the size of this house, right? There's plenty of room. There's a safe room in the basement that some of my teammates can sleep in and Roxanne and I will leave the day after tomorrow. We have a little guy to get home to."

Her mom immediately picked up on that one. "Oh, how old is he?"

Hawk beamed. "He's twenty months and walking every-where. Sophie's probably exhausted."

"Who's Sophie?"

"One of my teammates and a very good friend. She has a little guy of her own."

Roxanne turned to her parents. "We have plenty of room and we've used this home as a home base before. Though it was GHOST who was here and not RAPTOR, but it's the same family. It'll be just fine."

Carmella entered the room. "Dinner will be in fifteen minutes."

Roxanne stood. "Thank you, Carmella."

She kissed Hawk then walked into the kitchen. Hope watched her enter the kitchen area and Carmella turned to her and they hugged.

"Oh, that's so sweet," she whispered.

Hawk grinned. "Carmella is the most wonderful person in the world, and she's been in Roxanne's life her whole life. It pains Roxanne that Carmella is miffed that we didn't bring Henry. It just wasn't the time. So we'll be coming back in a week or two so Carmella can spoil him."

Hope smiled at Hawk. "Aww, that is sweet."

Hawk stood and picked his laptop up off the table. "I'll be back in a bit."

Hope looked across the table at her parents. "Are you two alright?"

Her mom swallowed. "You won't be putting yourself in any danger Hope, will you?"

"I'll be careful, Mom."

Creed stood then and picked up his laptop. "I promise you I won't let her get involved in anything dangerous. She'll be supplying us with information, and we'll be doing the dangerous stuff."

Her mom smiled at Creed. He nodded and stepped away from the table. "I'll be right back." He squeezed her shoulder then walked around the table and to the foyer area under the stairs.

She watched until he'd disappeared then looked at her parents. "How are you two doing? I can see this has all taken a toll on you. Are you alright?"

Her father swallowed. "It's by far the worst thing to ever happen to us, Hope. I never want to go through anything like that again. Never."

Her mom's eyes welled with tears again and she smiled at her. "I thought about you all the time."

Her mom sobbed again, and Hope was sorry she'd made her cry.

30

Creed looked across the street at Byte Me's store front. It wasn't anything to speak of, a normal store wedged between two other normal stores, all three with the same brick façade. The only thing different about Byte Me was the neon sign in the window with the big mouth and teeth over the word Byte. Clever. If you're fourteen.

"I haven't seen anyone go in there for the past thirty minutes."

"Me either," Hawk responded.

"I'm going in. My comm unit is on. If he's alone, I'll let you know and we'll have words with him."

"Roger." Hawk inserted his earpiece and Creed stepped out of the SUV.

As he neared the store, he regulated his breathing. He was already pissed off at this Justin character, but he needed to remain cool to gather the information he needed.

Taking a deep breath just before entering the store made him feel better, but his stomach was still in knots.

The store was dumpy and the black electronics that lay on the shelves wore a coating of dust from years of sitting.

"Hey man, can I help you?"

He turned to see a thin reedy man sitting behind a counter to his right. He wore headphones, though the headphone over his left ear was now pulled down. He had stringy blond hair; the tips of it were colored green.

"Yeah. I'm looking for Justin."

"You got him."

Creed stepped closer to the counter and looked directly into Justin's eyes.

"I was sent here by Congressman Compton to pick up a recording you made from an audio brought in by Hope Dumond."

Justin's mouth opened and closed, then opened again. His eyes rounded and he dropped his hands to his lap.

"I don't know what you're talking about."

"That's not what the congressman told me. He emphatically said he wanted that recording. And the original. And that you have it."

"But I gave it to his man a few days ago."

"Well, he didn't get it. So far as he knows, you still have it."

"I swear I don't. I gave it to the man he sent."

"What was the man's name?"

"Aah, um," He picked up a well-worn notebook and thumbed through the pages. "Here, see, ten days ago Connor Fitzjarrell came in to pick up the audio file for the congressman."

Creed's eyebrows rose into his hairline. "Did he show you ID?"

Justin's brows drew together and he shook his head. "No, the congressman called and said he was sending Connor Fitzjarrell over in an hour."

"How did you give him the files?"

Justin clenched his jaw and leaned in close. That was the motivation he needed.

"I gave him a thumb drive because the congressman didn't want anything sent through the servers and he didn't want a ghost trace left on his computer."

Creed took a deep breath and looked around, then looked directly at Justin. "Apparently you haven't heard the news, but Connor Fitzjarrell was found dead ten days ago."

"I had nothing to do with that. I was here. All day, I was here. See?" He shoved his dirty notebook across the counter, "Look, I had other customers that day. After Fitzjarrell was here."

Creed clenched his jaw and the door opened. Hawk entered the store and Justin looked like his breakfast was about to make a reappearance.

"Justin here says he knows nothing about Fitzjarrell and that he gave Fitzjarrell the audio."

"That so." Hawk puffed out his chest and looked into the scrawny man's eyes.

Hawk glanced at Creed. "You know what we have to do now, right?"

"Yeah. I'll lock the door."

"Wait. I don't have it. I gave it to Fitz..." Justin stood from the stool he had been perched on and looked right and left. He held both hands up, palms facing Hawk and him and his bottom lip quivered.

"I have a copy. I kept..." He swallowed. "I have one here."

"Let's hear it. Keep your hands where we can see them."

Justin sat on his stool, his fingers shook as he started to rest them on the keyboard, but he halted. "I have to type."

"Turn your monitor around so I can see what you're typing."

Justin turned his monitor, moved some items on the counter then moved it again so they could see what he was typing.

He clicked with his mouse a few times, entering files, then a folder on the screen said, "Hope D." Creed's jaw tightened, and Justin clicked on the folder to reveal audio files. There appeared to be fifteen or so and were in both MP3 and MOV files.

"Play the first one."

Justin clicked on the first one and the voice of a male could be heard making a deal. "I'll wire you the money from the account once it's removed. Where will the assets be?"

"I'll have them on the boat at the marina. *The Money Maker.*"

That second voice wasn't Dilano, he knew that much.

"Click on the others."

One by one Justin played clips for Creed and Hawk to hear.

"I want them copied onto this thumb drive immediately." Creed produced a thumb drive that would also wipe Justin's computer free of the files upon completion.

Justin's voice shook when he responded. "It'll take a little while, some of the clips are long."

"I don't care. Get a start on it."

"Okay...okay. What time will you be back for it?"

Hawk laughed and Creed grinned. "We're sitting right here until we get the copy."

Justin swallowed and his shaking fingers managed to insert the thumb drive into his computer. He started to move his monitor back, but Hawk stuck out his hand and held the monitor in place, then shook his head.

Justin swallowed again and began clicking the files and copying them over. Creed and Hawk watched as the computer showed them the files copying from the computer to the thumb drive. Hawk nodded to Creed.

"I'll go get my laptop."

Creed nodded but watched the files and Justin's fingers to make sure nothing untoward was happening.

Raising his phone, he tapped Caiden's picture and held his phone to his ear.

Caiden answered on the first ring. "Are you ready?"

"Yes. Copying is taking place as we speak."

"Got it. With the thumb drive in, I can access and transfer the files to our server. Hang tight while I log in."

Creed watched Justin closely and Hawk reentered the store within a couple of minutes. He made a show of opening his laptop on the counter in front of Justin and logging into his computer. Justin watched the much larger man type and at a minimum had an idea that Hawk wasn't just the muscle here.

Justin's eyes darted between Hawk and himself and he watched the files on the computer transfer over. Caiden chuckled. "Got it. Got all of them. Don't know what operating system he's using, but it's slow as fuck."

Creed chuckled. "You geeks are all alike."

Caiden laughed then, "You mean good in the sack?"

"Not exactly." Creed grinned and shook his head and Justin sat like a stone now that he had each of the files transferring. At one point, he lifted his hands to the keyboard and Creed shook his head. "No!" Which halted Justin's progress immediately. Hawk heaved out a deep breath and Justin looked at him and swallowed.

As the last file finished, Hawk held out his hand for the thumb drive and Justin shakily pulled it from his computer and handed it over.

Hawk inserted the thumb drive into his laptop and Caiden said, "Finished."

Creed looked at the folder on Justin's computer and the files were all gone. Hope's folder was gone too, and the screen reverted to his main screen.

"Hey, what the fuck just happened?"

"Nothing more than you deserve you little son of a bitch. Did you call Congressman Compton and rat out Hope Dumond?"

"I did…" Hawk stood taller once again and Justin swallowed. "She was recording him."

"Do you realize he tried to have her killed because of you?"

"He wouldn't do that. He's a good…"

"Right."

He left the store with Hawk, the ride back to the Bowman home was quiet but it was an easy quiet. A mile out Hawk glanced at him. "You love her?"

"I don't know."

Hawk chuckled. "I get it."

"Did you love Roxanne right away?"

One shoulder rose and fell and he scratched the side of his face. "Now I'd say yes, but to be honest I don't know. I thought she was stunning, but she was a pain in my ass. She had loads of sass and she kept trying to run away from me. But I didn't let her get away. I told myself it was the mission. Then I went home without her. I hated every second of my time without her. Then she came for Dodge and Jax's wedding and the instant I saw her, I knew I'd never let her go. Even if it meant I'd have to move to this shithole of a city."

He nodded as he absorbed what Hawk had to say. Hope didn't have a ton of sass, but she'd been through an ordeal that many would have crumbled from. She was strong. She was working through it all.

"Then how did you know you loved Roxanne?"

Hawk turned to him and studied his profile for a while. After a few moments he sat back in the seat and took a deep breath. "I didn't want to wake up in the morning if she wasn't in my life. When I looked at her, I could see her in my life forever. When I thought about the future, I wanted her there to experience all the things."

He pulled the SUV into the garage and shut it off. "Thanks Hawk."

Hawk shrugged. "Anytime."

As he walked to the house, his thoughts were on where he went from here. He wanted Hope. He liked her and wanted to keep her safe. And, somewhere along the way, that became less about the job and more about wanting her to be safe.

Opening the door, the house was quiet, the kitchen was dark and no food was cooking. Hope walked into the kitchen, her hands locked together in worry, her eyes locked on his.

"Is everything alright?"

"Yes. We wiped Justin's computer; he had the audio files in a folder named 'Hope D."

Hawk opened the fridge and pulled out a bottle of water. "Did Roxanne go to bed?"

"Yeah. My parents too."

"Then I'll say goodnight."

Hawk left the room and he stared at Hope for a while. Yeah, he loved looking at her. "Are you tired?"

She smiled. "Yeah."

He moved to stand in front of her, his right hand cupped her jaw as his eyes looked into hers. Her arms wrapped around his waist and pulled him tightly to her and his heart skipped a beat. He bent his head and kissed her lips softly, but she deepened the kiss.

She was so small against him. Frail. But, hopefully very soon he'd have her healthy and strong again as in the pictures he'd found of her on social media. Piper and Caiden had worked up a beautiful file on Hope and he wanted to know that Hope. She was always laughing. Vivacious and lively. He was going to heal her to her old self again. Softly, he nipped at her lips, tasted her. The lingering hint of sweet wine on her tongue beckoned him and he slid his tongue along hers. The feel of them together damned near made him dizzy. His right hand slid up her back and cupped the back of her head as his tilted to fit their lips together.

Her breathing grew choppy, her fingers shook as they splayed across his back. He nipped at her bottom lip and felt her shiver.

He bent his knees and wrapped his arms lower around her, then stood, lifting her feet off the ground. She wrapped her legs around his waist. The skirt she wore halted her progress and she quickly reached down and lifted it over her knees then wrapped her legs around him. His cock roared to life, his blood pulsed so fast and furious through his veins he felt his body heat. His lips sought hers once again and her hands held his head on either side as he carried her to the stairs.

He gently set her feet on the ground. "In case your parents happen to come out of their room."

"Yeah."

She took his hand and began climbing the steps which at this moment felt like Mount Everest. She quietly turned the handle on their door and slipped inside, pulling him gently in with her.

Hope pulled her denim jacket off her body and let it fall behind him. Four more steps and his knees felt the bed. Lifting his right leg to place his knee on the bed, he whispered in her ear, "I'm clean, Hope." He'd give her an out if she wanted it.

She froze for a moment and looked into his eyes. "I am too. At least I'm pretty sure. I haven't been with anyone in more than a year."

"A year?"

"I've been working a lot."

He kissed her lips lightly. "Me too."

He didn't move to lay her down. Her eyes locked on his and neither of them moved.

Slowly, she ran her hands through his short beard, her thumb swiped over his bottom lip. His tongue reached out and licked her thumb, then sucked it into his mouth and suckled it gently.

She pulled it out slowly then touched her lips to his once more; this time their kiss blazed and their hands roamed.

He laid her down on the bed, but instead of lying on her, he stood and removed his clothing. She may as well see him without his leg. She may have a change of heart. It was always a fear, lingering in the back of his mind, that someone wouldn't find him attractive once they saw him as he really was without his prosthetic. In his mind he was whole, but when he looked in the mirror, he wasn't.

He pulled his shirt over his head and watched as Hope pulled her skirt down her hips as she lifted off the bed, then slipped it down her sexy slender legs. He swallowed as he unbuttoned his khakis and slid the zipper down, then let them drop to the floor. Stepping out of them, he watched her eyes. He could feel them roam over his body like they had fingers of their own. His skin heated everywhere her eyes landed.

Hope sat up, licked her lips, then pulled her top over her head and let it fall to the floor. He marveled at her body. Her ribs were prominent, but soon they'd be covered in more flesh. Her skin was flawless, she had no scars, other than her wrists. He hesitated as he looked at the near perfection before him.

She lifted herself to a sitting position, reached behind her and unhooked her bra. Her breasts spilled from the fabric as she removed it, and she made a show of dropping it to the floor, a saucy smile on her lips.

He inhaled deeply and tucked his thumbs into his boxer briefs, then slid them over his hips, his cock standing tall and firm. He turned and sat on the bed, then slowly, slipped his thumbs into his prosthesis and slipped it from his natural leg. He tugged the stocking off the stub and took a deep breath before turning to see Hope's face.

She moved to the edge of the bed and stood. She shimmied her panties over her hips and legs and let them drop to the floor where the rest of their clothing rested.

Hope stepped to him, her body directly in front of his. Her left breast in alignment with his lips, so he sucked her nipple into his mouth.

Her hands held his head, his hands wrapped around her body and pulled her as close as he could. Switching to her right breast he suckled it and enjoyed the sweet noises of pleasure she made.

She pulled back slightly; her hands slid down his head to his shoulders where she gently pushed him down on the bed. Her slender body laid on his, and his hands roamed over her. Squeezing and rubbing her skin, he enjoyed the feel of her ass in his hands, her body lying on his. She continued to kiss his lips, his jaw, his cheeks, and back to his lips.

He rolled them over so her body was under his and her legs wrapped around his hips, positioning him at her entrance.

"Are you sure?"

She whispered, "Yes."

Tightening his hips, he pushed slowly into her and they both moaned at the feeling. She was warmth enveloping him in satin. He pulled out and pushed in again, and that same feeling washed over his body. A shiver skittered down his spine as he entered her again, her eyes locked on his, her lips parted perfectly into an "O" as he entered her again.

Dipping his head, he licked her lips then kissed her nose and entered her again.

Her hips rose as he plunged into her over and over and both of them were coated in a fine sheen of sweat as she cried out his name. He thrust twice more and let his orgasm flow into her body as his arms shook with the effort not to fall on her.

Hope's arms wrapped around his shoulders as he eased himself down, his lips kissed her jaw to her ear where he whispered, "Unreal. You feel unreal."

31

Hope's fingers twisted in her lap as she sat in the living room of the Bowman home. Her parents had gone upstairs to read and Hope was simply too wired to do the same. She'd tossed and turned all night from the events of the day. She lay tucked into Creed's side after they made love, but she hadn't asked him about what happened earlier and while she felt protected here, her life was anything but safe or settled in any way.

She inhaled deeply and let it out, watching a bee buzz along the top of a red flower in front of the window. It flitted from petal to petal, then flew to the next flower and did the same.

"You look lost in thought." Roxanne entered the room and sat in the armchair to her left.

"I am. Things are happening so fast I'm struggling to keep up and I'm nervous about everything."

"I understand that. When I met Hawk, it was right over there." She pointed to the foyer between this room and the office. "I thought he was breaking into my house, he thought I had broken in. Our first meeting was less than perfect. We struggled and fought and it took me a while to get over being pissed at him. My parents had just been murdered a couple weeks prior and I was reeling from that. Then, they sicced Jax on me."

"Who's Jax?"

Roxanne laughed. "Now, she's one of my closest friends. Then, she was a pissy, sassy, badass operative who informed me she didn't like babysitting."

"Oh. Wow. That sounds kind of terrifying."

"At the time I was too pissed off to be scared. Good thing I guess."

"I'm sorry to hear about your parents."

"Thank you. I miss them every day and I'm so sad they weren't here to meet Henry. But I'll always tell Henry about them. He'll know them through me."

She smiled at Roxanne. "That's wonderful."

The back door opened and Carmella's voice floated out to them. "Hello, Mr. Hawk and Mr. Creed, did you have a nice workout?"

"Hi, Carmella, we sure did." Hawk responded.

"Hi, Carmella. It smells wonderful in here as always."

"Oh Mr. Creed, you're too kind."

Creed chuckled and Hope scooted to the edge of the sofa. Their footsteps grew louder and Hope's heart beat faster.

Creed appeared around the doorway, sweat dripping down his temples, his shirt dampened with sweat and looked he directly at her. "Hey, there."

"Hi."

Roxanne looked back and smiled at her husband, who was equally sweaty but quick to kiss her lips.

Creed sat next to her and Hawk occupied the second armchair next to Roxanne.

"I didn't get to ask you how it went yesterday? You left this morning before I could ask you about it."

"We have the audio files. And they're wiped from Justin's computer. And, he had given them to the Congressman and called him after you dropped them off."

"That. Fucker."

Hawk laughed and Creed's eyebrows rose into his hairline.

"Wow." Creed chuckled.

"Well, he...I could have been killed."

"Yes. What he did was awful. I don't think he realized what the congressman would do. But, he's paying for it now."

"Did you beat the shit out of him?"

Hawk laughed again. "We don't do that."

Her shoulders dropped. "Oh."

Creed grinned at her and took her hand in his. "Hawk used the scrambler and erased all the electronics in Justin's store. He's doing damage control on his customers' electronic devices right now and if that doesn't bankrupt him, we'll try again."

Hope looked into Creed's eyes. The grin on his face and light dancing in his eyes told her he loved this idea. "I guess that's probably better than breaking his fingers."

Hawk chuckled. "Trust me, it'll be more painful than broken fingers."

Hawk turned to Roxanne, "Did you call Sophie?"

"Yes. Henry doesn't even know we're gone."

"Bullshit." Hawk burst out. "I miss that little man so much, he better know I'm gone."

Roxanne giggled. "He knows. But she's keeping him and Tate busy and we'll see him in the morning."

Creed's phone chimed. He pulled it from his pocket and read a text.

He glanced at Hawk. "Fitzjarrell owns the Caddy."

Hawk nodded. "You have an address?"

"Yep."

"Let's shower, grab lunch then go see what we can find out."

Creed stood and held his hand out to her. "Who's Fitzjarrell?"

"Not only the man that followed your parents, but the one Justin gave the recordings to."

Hawk and Roxanne stood and Roxanne turned toward the dining room, while Hawk jogged up the stairs. Creed pulled her into his arms then pulled away. She grinned and wrapped her arms around his waist and pulled him tightly to her. "Did you sleep well last night?"

His arms wrapped tightly around her, and his cheek rested on the top of her head. "I did, how about you?"

"I didn't. My mind raced with all that had gone on. Or may have gone on and I'll be honest, I made it all so much darker in my mind."

He chuckled. "We aren't thugs but we do manage to get our point across."

She giggled. "I know. I guess I've seen too many mob movies and been through something I never dreamed I'd be involved in, so my head went...there."

He kissed the top of her head. "I'll be back down in five minutes."

"I'll run up and let my parents know it's almost time for breakfast."

"I'll see you at the table."

He swatted her on the butt as she passed him. She squealed lightly but she smiled all the way up the stairs. Especially since he followed her and every time she glanced at him, he was staring at her.

She turned toward her parents' room and he disappeared into their room.

At her soft knock her father sleepily answered, "Come in."

Cracking the door open, she stuck her head inside. "Carmella has something delicious-smelling ready for breakfast if you're hungry."

Her father sat up and rubbed his eyes. "Yes, I'm hungry. Did Creed and Hawk come back?"

"Yes, last night, they just came back from a hard workout a few minutes ago. Come on down and they'll fill you in."

Her mom sat up and ran her fingers through her hair. It was lighter than Hope's, a sandy blonde, and she wore it in a bob. She'd had that same hairstyle for as long as Hope could remember. But it suited her, and her mom always said it was so easy to maintain.

Hope smiled at her parents. "I love you guys."

Her mom stood and embraced her in a tight hug. "We love you too, baby. So very much."

32

Fitzjarrell lived in a upper-middle class neighborhood. The homes were all brick and had extensively landscaped lawns. According to the report that Cyber had compiled, he wasn't married and had no children. His home was in the middle of the block on the south side, but the backyards of that side of the street were densely wooded.

Creed inched passed Fitzjarrell's house, then stopped at the end of the street. "Go in the back?"

"Yes. It seems quiet, but you never know who's watching with all the security cameras on everyone's doors these days. Let's put caps on and keep your head down."

Creed drove to the opposite end of the street and parked the SUV at a little park on the edge of the woods.

He pulled a blue cap from his duffle bag, with no advertising on it, nothing that would make it stand out. Hawk pulled a dark green cap from his bag and pulled it on his head, tugging on the brim to lower it on his forehead.

They exited the SUV and entered the woods. He pulled his phone out and tapped on the GPS and then the hiking app. They managed through the dense trees and downed branches fairly easy. As they neared Fitzjarrell's backyard, they stopped at the edge and looked at the backyards on either side of his home.

Hawk pulled the scrambler from his bag and turned it on. He watched it until a green light flashed on his screen then he nodded. "Okay."

They dashed across the backyard, making their way to the side door of the garage. Creed slid the keying device into the lock and jiggled it in place to unlock the door. He and Hawk slipped inside and waited for their eyes to adjust to the darkened garage.

Noting the door to the house across the garage, they quietly edged along the room, noting one car, the Caddy, was missing. The other two stalls held a convertible Mustang and a truck.

Creed tried the handle on the door and found it to be unlocked. They slipped inside.

Moving through the darkened house, Creed led them down a hallway, looking for an office. The first room past the living room was it. Slipping inside, Creed opened the laptop laying on the desk and Hawk began searching through drawers and shelving to find a thumb drive or other portable device.

Creed inserted a device into the USB port on the laptop and texted Caiden. Within a minute, Caiden responded, "Running a password scanner now."

While that was running, he helped Hawk search in the desk drawers and files. It was more than likely that the congressman now had custody, but he'd bet his left nut that Fitzjarrell made copies for himself. It was insurance when dealing with people like this. It was also deadly.

His phone buzzed and he glanced at it. "All set. It's unlocked."

Grabbing the mouse lying on the desk, he clicked on the search bar and typed in "Hope D." The search turned up nothing, so he tried "Compton."

A folder opened up and he clicked through it but found nothing pertaining to Hope or the audio. He tried another search, "Compton audio."

That pulled up a folder named "Protection."

"No honor among thieves, Hawk."

"Find it?"

"Yeah."

Creed clicked on the folder and saw the audio files. He copied them to the thumb drive then texted Caiden. "Copied all files to the thumb drive."

"Got them. Deleting."

He watched as the files disappeared from Fitzjarrell's protection file but didn't feel bad about the fact that his protection just vanished. He closed the lid on the laptop, and they exited the office, then quickly stepped out into the garage. Slipping from the side door they quickly walked toward the woods and disappeared inside them, hidden from view of anyone watching.

Retracing their path to the SUV they exited the woods about a hundred yards from a group of younger boys smoking a joint. When he looked over at them, one of them gave him the finger and the others laughed. Fuckers.

He turned to the SUV and walked as quickly as he could without looking suspicious. Just as they started driving down the street, the Cadillac came into view, and it neared its street.

"Heads up." He warned Hawk.

Hawk looked down at his lap, his green cap still on his head.

He stared straight ahead as the Caddy met them on the road and didn't detect that Fitzjarrell had noticed him at all. Letting out a sigh of relief, he continued through the neighborhood and made his way toward the Bowman home.

Both his phone and Hawk's began pinging and Hawk pulled up the messages he was receiving. He chuckled and turned his phone toward him showing a picture of Falcon in a suit and tie and Kori wearing a pretty dress.

"Says, "I'm married, fuckers.""

Creed burst out laughing. "Typical Falcon."

Hawk chuckled. "Yep. Then there's this one from Ford. "I have a new daughter. She's just as messy as the little one." Hawk twisted his hand once more to show a picture of Kori stuffing a piece of wedding cake into Falcon's mouth. Crumbs all over the front of Falcon's suit.

He turned onto the back street behind the Bowman home; Hawk opened the garage door and he pulled the SUV inside. His phone continued to ping as messages came in from Falcon. Then Emmy. Piper sent a couple. Charly sent more. Each of his teammates wanted him to know they were thinking of him, and dammit that felt good.

They entered the house at the back door and Hope stood in the doorway between the kitchen and the foyer.

"Hi."

He smiled at her and turned his phone around so she could see the pictures. "Falcon and Kori are married."

They scrolled through the pictures as Hawk did the same, with Roxanne sitting next to him at the dining room table. He kissed Hope's temple and put his arm around her. "They look happy."

She giggled. "They do. Both of them look as though they've healed nicely."

"Yeah, they're tough."

Falcon sent another text then, "We'll be in at eight tomorrow morning. Kori and I, Emmy, Charly, Diego, and Van."

"Okay. We'll be at the airport to pick you up and deliver Hawk and Roxanne to fly back."

33

Hope climbed into bed next to Creed. He held his arm out to wrap her in tight and she nestled into his side with a sigh.

"You make me feel so safe."

He grunted slightly and rolled to his side to face her.

"I love that you feel safe with me Hope. But, for us to last, you're going to need to feel safe on your own too."

"I know. My parents have been telling me that too. And, before that I knew it. I don't know how to get there."

"It takes time. What you went through was traumatic. And, once we have the congressman, his wife, and his cohorts off the streets and in prison, you should see a therapist to help you manage your healing."

She knew she should, and her parents had offered to pay for it. "Yeah. Mom said she'd help me find someone. It'll likely need to be somewhere out of this city."

"That's a good idea. And, certainly something that doesn't need to be decided right now. I just want us to be realistic."

She looked into his eyes. What she saw there was honesty. He stared into her eyes for a long time, a slow smile creased his face. "I love looking at you. You are so beautiful."

She smiled. "I love looking at you. You are the handsomest man I've ever met."

He leaned in and kissed her lips and it felt so good. So right. They fit perfectly together. The way her body fit into his was perfection on its own. Her nipples tightened as his hand floated down her hip then slid across her butt cheek and squeezed. His lips continued to mold against hers and his tongue slid along hers. He tasted of the bourbon he'd just had with Hawk. He smelled of the woodsy scent she'd grown to love. He felt like a god, all firm ridges and planes as her hands roamed through and over them.

He gently laid her back and climbed over her body. His lips kissed a delicious path down her jaw, then her neck and over her collarbone, stopping and nipping then kissing along the path he'd just lit on fire.

Once back to her lips, he repeated his sweet kisses on the other side, then back once again. His head dipped down, with a kiss along the underside of her chin, then down her throat to her right breast where he sucked her in. She gasped as he sucked her. The feeling so intense her toes curled.

He kissed across her chest to her left breast, and she gasped again as he sucked her deep into his mouth. She raised her legs and crossed her ankles at the base of his back, lifting her hips as much as she could to add the friction she needed.

He let her breast fall from his mouth, then kissed back up her neck and to her lips.

"I want you inside of me."

He groaned and lifted himself slightly and reached between them to position his cock at her entrance. The feel of his hardness against her was exciting. Remembering how he felt the first time, her excitement grew once more. Tilting her hips, she tried urging him inside, but he nibbled along her jaw to her ear.

"This is my favorite part," he whispered.

He pushed himself inside of her, but only the head of his cock entered her. He pulled out, then repeated the same movement and pulled out once more. The third time he pushed into her, he went in deeper and she gasped.

Once again, he repeated his motion and pushed in deeper. Her arms wrapped tightly around his shoulders; her legs squeezed him to her. The anticipation of him moving faster was beginning to frustrate her. She wanted him now.

"Creed."

"Isn't this the best?"

"No. The best is when you're all the way inside of me."

"I beg to differ." He nipped her ear once again and pulled out then pushed in nice and slow.

She whispered near his ear. "That's the best. God, that. Is. My. Favorite. Feeling."

He chuckled slightly then increased his pace, pulling out and pushing in, repeating over and over. She tried being quiet. Her parents were in the next room. But, he. Felt. So. Good.

She matched his moves. Their mating dance was beautiful. He was beautiful. Each time he filled her completely, she grew closer to her orgasm. He lifted his head to look into her eyes.

"I want to watch you."

Her skin heated. Her heart beat rapidly. Her body was on fire.

Her hips rose to meet him again and again. She gasped as her orgasm rolled over her and he quieted her with his lips. He caught her pleasure in his mouth then kissed her lips beautifully as she came down from her orgasm.

"You okay?" he asked as he looked into her eyes.

"Better."

"Good."

His pace increased and it didn't take more than a few strokes before his orgasm erupted, his head dropped into the pillow alongside her head as he gasped and groaned. Her hands held his head, her legs held his body. Her heart beat wildly against his. They lay that way for a few minutes as their bodies cooled and their heartbeats returned to normal.

He slid off her, grabbed tissues from the bedside table and handed her some. She went into the bathroom to clean herself up. Her knees still shook but the smile on her face couldn't be wiped off for anything.

When she climbed back into bed, his arms reached for her and quickly wrapped her in a safe cocoon. She drifted off listening to his steady even breathing and smelling his delicious woodsy scent and knowing that she'd found her one and only. Her heart knew it. She just had to make sure she was healthy enough to make it work. She felt like she was. And she'd work for it, no matter what it took.

34

C reed shook Hawk's hand and gave him a brief hug.

"Thanks for your help, man."

"Anytime."

Hawk hugged Hope while he hugged Roxanne. "Thank you for the use of your home. We'll take care of it."

Her smile was brilliant. "I have no doubt."

Hawk reached out and took Roxanne's hand. They walked to the airplane, chatting and smiling.

Falcon nudged him, "Ready?"

"Yeah." He held his hand out to Hope and walked with her to the SUV where Emmy, Diego, Van, and Charly waited for them.

Kori and Falcon were behind them, chatting softly with each other and he realized what it was that struck him when he looked at couples. They had things to chat about.

Nothing in particular, but couples that enjoyed each other liked talking to each other. They liked being together. That was what made the loneliness go away. That person who got you.

He opened the back door and helped Hope inside as Falcon and Kori made their way to the passenger side. Falcon kissed Kori before she hopped up into the SUV and he regretted not kissing Hope before she climbed inside. It was still too new.

He slid into the driver's seat and buckled up. Looking in his mirror, he saw Kori and Hope in the backseat and Emmy and Charly, in the third row of seats. Van, Diego, and Caiden were in the second SUV.

One of the SUVs would need to sit outside at the house, which could be a security risk.

He looked in the mirror at Emmy. "Do you think we should find a secure garage to keep one of the vehicles when it's not in use? The Dumonds' vehicle is in the second stall of the garage."

Emmy nodded. "Yes. We should actually store the Dumond's vehicle until it's safe for them to be out and about. Until then, they'll be with us if they leave the house."

Charly pulled her phone up. "I'll find something."

Creed's eyes darted quickly to Hope's behind him, and she smiled. He watched her swallow and realized she was likely nervous being out in public, but she was with them and it was good for her to get out again.

Emmy spoke up. "Let's go over a few things. Once we get to the house, we'll need to get to work asap. Hope, I need you to call Deacon and Piper and work with them on the list of names and phone numbers you had stored. Who are these people and what was the nature of the phone calls you managed to capture? They've compiled files on each of them, but we need to put them into proper perspective."

Hope turned to Emmy. "Okay."

"I asked Piper to set up a laptop for you so you can see the files we have on this mission. I have it in my suitcase and will get it to you as soon as we get to the house. You'll have access to add information once each person's profile is set up. If you think of something after speaking with Deacon and Piper, you can make a note."

"Okay."

"Creed. As soon as we have the profiles compiled, I'd like you to meet with the congressman as a buyer of Russian women. You'll go in wired and solidify a deal. We want to know when the women are coming into the country. Where they'll be brought in. When you'll gain custody and how money will be exchanged. Cyber managed to intercept some communication from one of the phone numbers Hope had. They attached crawlers to each of the phone numbers and listened for any chatter. One of them seems to be a buyer. His name is Merchi Sorenson. He's a new player, only been in the game for three months or so. This is his first buy. He set an appointment to meet Congressman Compton at a bar named The Filibuster on Front Street. They've never met, so you'll show in his place."

"Roger."

Emmy looked at her phone. "Falcon, you'll make sure Merchi Sorenson doesn't make it to the meeting."

"Roger."

Emmy continued, "Once we have the information Creed manages to get from the congressman, Roxanne will have her father's best friend, Wade, and some officers from the State Department there to arrest the congressman. It'll be a bonus if the wife shows up too. We'll grab them both. If she doesn't show up, we'll have officers go to the house and pick her up at the same time."

Hope turned around to Emmy. "I have notes hidden in the congressional building."

"We'll get them after the congressman is arrested. It's too dangerous to go in there before. He'll be tight-lipped and afraid to make another deal. Right now, he knows you aren't dead. But he doesn't know where you are."

"How do you know?"

"He isn't here. He's due to fly in from Florida this afternoon. Piper did a little investigating for us down there and found out he was in town. He flew in on a private plane, owned by none other than Anton Smith."

Kori turned to Emmy, "How can his plane still fly around wherever it wants to go? He could be inside for all authorities know."

"Right. But unfortunately the authorities, in this case the CIA, don't have carte blanche to search his plane without confirmation that he's on board. They are watching the airport though and saw the congressman exit the plane. Alone."

"Where did he go?"

"We haven't been given that information yet. I've requested it, but so far they aren't sharing."

Kori turned back to the front just as Creed pulled into the garage. Emmy slowly managed to make her way toward the open door.

He winced as he watched the deliberation of her movements. "Still in pain, Em?"

"Yes."

"You're going to need to meet Kori's doctor friend. What do you have to lose?"

She let out a long breath. "I know. I just need to be on this mission to bring this group down. We've been tailing them for two years now."

"It's not worth it if you're unable to walk, Em."

"It is. It's worth everything. Even my ability to walk."

He swallowed the lump in his throat. One thing was certain, Emmy's heart and soul were in this job. No one would ever be able to say otherwise.

35

Hope finished her phone call with Deacon and Piper and she felt exhausted. Remembering all of the names and when she'd first heard of them and what she suspected them to be doing with the congressman took a toll. She sat in the office of the Bowman home at Mrs. Bowman's desk. Directly across from her was Mr. Bowman's desk on the opposite side of the room. It was stately and elegant and she felt small in here. The tall windows allowed sunlight to stream in which made the room cheery and inviting, but the sheer size of the furniture was massive. Of course it would have to be in this home, everything here was large. And it was formal. So formal. She glanced out the nearest window to her and watched the birds fighting at the bird feeder. They flew around, landed, then took off when another bird nipped or opened its wings in warning. Watching all the food they tossed onto the ground made her shake her head. There was plenty for everyone with all the food laying in the landscaping.

"You look lost in thought."

She jumped at his voice then smiled when Creed smiled at her.

"I was just watching those little pigs toss birdseed on the ground then get mad at other birds when they try to eat from the feeder."

He looked outside the window and chuckled when two birds squawked and screeched at each other.

"They are testy little things."

Creed sat in one of the chairs facing Mrs. Bowman's desk and smiled at her.

"How did your call go?"

"Good. Tiring. I hope I remember everything I need to, so you get those assholes."

"So far, you've given us a great deal. And Emmy just said with the recordings and the notes you have hidden in the congressional building, plus some of the lowlifes you had phone numbers for, we'll have plenty of evidence to convict them."

"Coupled with the information you'll gather going into your meeting with the congressman."

He nodded. "Yes. With that."

She swallowed a dry knot that formed in her throat. "Are you scared?"

He shook his head. "Not of getting hurt. Only of not being able to get the information I need to get."

"I don't want you to get hurt."

"I won't, Hope. I'll be fine. Falcon, Charly, Diego, and Van will be close should things go bad."

"You all are amazing."

He laughed then and she stared at his face. He was handsome all the time. But, when he laughed, wow, he was stunning.

Her parents entered the office. "There you two are. How did your phone call go?"

"It went well. I can leave notes in their system if I remember something else."

Her mom smiled at her. "That's good, dear."

"How are you two doing? I know you aren't used to being cooped up. Even though this is a spectacular place to be cooped up in."

"It's fine honey. Carmella showed me how she made her Bolognese sauce. And we made homemade spaghetti noodles. Your father helped."

"That's nice."

"Wait till you taste it. It's so yummy. She's a spectacular cook. Tomorrow we're making a triple chocolate cake."

Her stomach growled and she giggled. "That sounds fantastic."

"It will be. Anyway, it's time for dinner."

"Okay." She glanced at Creed as her parents left the room.

He stood and waited for her to join him, then he wrapped her in a hug and held her close. "You did a great job today. You did a great thing keeping those names and phone numbers. I'm sure there were times when you wished you hadn't, but I'm glad you did."

"There was never a time when I wished I hadn't; only wished that someone would be able to use them for the purpose of putting them in jail. I'd hoped if I died, it wouldn't be for naught."

She heard him intake a deep breath and he squeezed her closer. She turned her head so her ear was over his heart and closed her eyes as she listened to it beat. Strong. Solid. Comforting.

"Shall we go eat?"

Opening her eyes she nodded but didn't move for a moment. She wanted to soak up his warmth and strength for a little while longer.

Too soon her stomach growled again, and she pulled away from his body. He took her hand and led her to the dining room where the rest of his teammates and her parents sat waiting for them. He held Hope's chair for her to his right, then took the seat at the head of the table, opposite her father. Kole nodded as he sat down, and Carmella began bringing the food into the room.

Falcon sat to his left and was the first to comment. "Damn I'm going to love staying here. That smells amazing."

Emmy laughed. "I'm telling Sheldon you said that."

"I'll deny it."

Charly snickered. "I'm a witness. So is Creed."

She looked at Creed. "Who's Sheldon?"

"He's our chef at home."

"You have a chef?"

"We do. And he's an amazing chef, but he focuses on the healthier variety of food."

Carmella stopped in her tracks. "My food is healthy."

Creed's eyes rounded. "I didn't mean that, Carmella. I meant, Sheldon focuses on less meat and pasta and more vegetables and protein."

"Hmm," she said as she continued on into the kitchen.

Charly chuckled. "You made her mad now. Tomorrow we'll have fish and veggies."

Her mom looked down the table. "We're making triple chocolate cake tomorrow."

"Gah, I can't remember the last time I had triple chocolate cake."

Falcon laughed. "You'll go home round and poor Sam won't let you go on a mission again."

Emmy shook her head. "Sam would adore Charly if she weighed a ton. That man looks at her with love in his eyes."

Hope added some of the pasta and Bolognese to her plate and half-listened to the chatter at the table. It felt so carefree to eat a regular meal. Her appetite was back and she hoped Creed would love her if she grew rounder. She stopped with her fork almost to her mouth. Like. She hoped he'd like her. He didn't love her. They weren't there. Yet.

36

Creed walked down the grand staircase with his suit on. The wire had been inserted into the lapel, invisible to everyone. The tiny Bluetooth control was embedded into the liner of the jacket and controlled by a button on the suit. Ingenious little device.

He walked to the dining room where most of the group sat, either on their computers or, in the case of Kole and Carolyne Dumond, reading.

Diego chuckled. "You almost look respectable."

Creed glanced at the Dumonds at the end of the table and didn't say what he wanted to, but he did give Diego the finger, which was hidden from the Dumonds by Charly's head.

Charly turned and looked first at his middle finger then at his suit. She grinned. "I think you look nice. Wanna test the wire?"

"Yeah. I would."

Charly stood and left the room with her phone and Creed glanced at Hope across the table. Her eyes locked on his and his heart beat a bit faster. Her soft smile did more to bolster his determination to get those guys than he'd like to admit.

"You look very handsome, Creed."

Nodding, his eyes darted to her parents then back to Hope. Carolyne nodded. "You do look very handsome."

His cheeks heated and Hope's smile grew. It was beautiful.

His phone buzzed. A text from Charly. "Ready."

He replied with a thumbs up, then touched the button on his jacket as he sat in her vacated chair at the table.

"Emmy, did Roxanne call Wade about this afternoon?"

"She did. He'll be ready. Actually, he'll have officers ready. They'll be patrons sitting at tables while you're at the Filibuster."

"Good. And the congressman will be arrested, provided I can get the details such as finalizing a deal? When the women are arriving? Where they are now? Where they'll be delivered? How much money?"

"Yes. And we've managed to transcribe Hope's recordings. Seems the going rate for Russian women is $300,000 per woman or a million two for four."

Hope turned her head toward Emmy. "I'm not saying a life should be reduced to dollars and cents, but I'm shocked they're willing to pay three hundred thousand."

Emmy nodded and turned to look at Hope. "It appears it's based on age. Under eighteen, say fourteen years old is the most popular age. They figure the average life span of the girls is eight to ten years. They either escape or die of drug use. On the low end, at eight years, the three hundred thousand breaks down to thirty-seven thousand five hundred dollars. These women are required, in most cases, to turn four tricks a day at one hundred dollars each. Over the course of eight years they will bring in close to one million two hundred thousand dollars. Three hundred thousand dollars to make over a million two is a good return on investment. The fact that they're from Russia usually means they'll be pimped out for more than one hundred dollars per trick. Plus they can't easily run home; they have nowhere else to go, so they stay longer. That's why they ship them."

Charly came bounding into the dining room. "It works great. I heard every word. Falcon, I even heard you typing."

Kori laughed. "That was me."

"Even better—you're further from Creed."

Hope's brows furrowed. "I thought you had to touch a button to make it work."

He grinned at her. "I did, when I sat down."

"Oh. I thought you were unbuttoning your jacket. Very smooth."

He nodded and grinned, then stood. "Ready Falcon? Charly? Diego? Van?"

"Yep." Falcon stood and closed the lid on his laptop. He leaned down and kissed Kori's lips then made his way around the dining room table. Charly stood to his right.

Creed smiled at Hope. He wanted to kiss her before he left. But her parents.

As if she could read his mind, Hope stood and walked toward him, and he leaned in and kissed her lips without hesitation. Her parents should get used to it. "I'll see you in a while."

"Please be careful."

"I will. You stay close to Emmy and Caiden so you'll be able to hear us. If you have any suggestions as you hear Compton talking, tell Emmy and she'll get a message to me."

"How?"

"She'll send me a text."

"Okay."

He nodded to the Dumonds, turned and walked with Charly, Diego, Van, and Falcon out of the dining room, to the kitchen, then out the back door to the garage. Van quietly said, "Get your head in the game, man."

"It's in the game."

"We all need to come back this afternoon. There'll be chocolate cake."

Charly laughed. "Triple chocolate cake."

Creed rubbed his belly. "Now that's something to come back for."

Charly shoved his shoulder as they entered the garage.

Falcon held up the keys, "I'm driving. You think about what you're going to say to Compton. For instance, what's your name?"

"Merchi Sorenson."

"Where are you from?"

"That isn't important. What's important is I have money and I'm in the market for girls."

"Who told you I have girls?"

"I never divulge my sources."

Falcon grinned as he turned onto the highway to take them to the Filibuster. "But, in case he insists?"

"Charly, what is the name of someone who has purchased from Compton before?"

She scrolled through her phone. "Andrew Bronwyn." She read quietly then continued, "He's made several deals with Compton. But after his last deal he was pissed off. The girls were older and Compton wanted the full three hundred thousand for them."

Creed nodded. "That could work in my favor. I can use that little tidbit to reinforce that I know Bronwyn."

Charly sat forward slightly. "Falcon, where will you be?"

"You pick Charly, do you want the front or the back door?"

"Wanna flip a coin?"

"Sure."

Creed pulled some change from his front pocket. "Okay, call it."

Charly called it first. "Heads."

Falcon looked in the mirror at her and shook his head. "That gives me tails."

Creed flicked the coin with his thumb and caught it between his hands, then slapped it on the back of his left hand and held his right hand over it. "Ready?"

Charly leaned closer and Falcon glanced over as Creed lifted his right hand.

"Heads it is."

Charly clapped her hands. "I'll take the front door. Van and Diego will take the parking lot."

37

Falcon parked them two blocks down and around the corner. Creed waited in the vehicle for Charly, Falcon, Van, and Diego to be in place to stop Merchi Sorenson before he entered the bar. And Creed wanted to wait until Compton was in the bar before he walked in. Best not to look too eager.

His comm unit clicked. "Charly in place."

Falcon replied soon. "Falcon in place."

"Van in place."

Finally, "Diego in place."

Creed took a deep breath and rotated his shoulders. His eyes scanned the street watching for anything or anyone that might be associated with Compton. The file he'd read mentioned Compton's wife, Helen Rathburg Compton, never joined him for these meetings.

His comm unit clicked again and Falcon said, "Compton entering the back door. Alone. Wearing a dark gray suit with a red tie."

"Roger."

Creed exited the SUV and walked to Front Street then turned right to head to the Filibuster. He told his team, "En route on Front Street."

As he neared the front door of the Filibuster, he spied Charly leaning against the wall, looking bored out of her mind. She didn't glance his way or make eye contact in case anyone was watching. She tucked a stray lock of hair behind her ear and looked in another direction.

Creed entered the Filibuster and was surprised it was empty. By empty, he meant empty. There wasn't even a bartender behind the bar. But Compton sat at a table in the middle of the room, looking in his direction. Compton's eyes were stone cold as he stared at Creed. Creed stared back with no facial emotion. Two could play this game.

He approached Compton's table and pulled out the chair directly across from him without being asked and sat, unbuttoning his jacket as he did.

"Name?"

"Merchi Sorenson."

"Where are you from?"

Upon close inspection, Compton had an extra chin and a bulbous nose. Winston Churchill came to mind based on pictures Creed had seen of him. Karl Malden as well. His shirt stretched across his abdomen, the buttons straining to stay in place. It was hard not to chuckle at the thought of all his buttons bursting free. He wasn't overly large, just a man who'd gained some weight and hadn't adjusted his clothing size to match. His hair was dark blond blended with streaks of gray. His file said he was fifty-four; his face said he was much older. Living in DC likely aged a person dealing in the swamp. Of which, Compton was one of the ugliest creatures of all. A trafficker.

"It doesn't matter where I'm from. It also doesn't matter where I'm going from here."

Compton stared at him for a long time. "What is it you want, Merchi Sorenson?"

"I'm looking for girls. At the moment about four."

"What makes you think that's something I have?"

"I have my sources. I think you know that, otherwise, why are we meeting?"

Compton stared. He sat stone still; it was so unusual to see someone so inanimate.

Finally, Compton cocked his head slightly. "We'll stop this meeting now unless you tell me who sent you to me."

Creed shrugged his right shoulder, then leaned back in his chair, and crossed his left ankle over his right leg.

"Andrew Bronwyn told me about your deals."

Compton half nodded. "Bronwyn." He spat.

Creed didn't respond as he watched Compton's eyes. They showed no emotion.

"So, you say you want girls. What kind of girls?"

"Russian girls. Young."

He ignored the disgust he felt in his stomach even acting like this was normal.

"Why Russian?"

"They bring more money and are easier to keep in line."

Compton chuckled then. "Yes. That's what I've found myself."

Creed remained quiet and unmoving.

Compton sat forward. It was the first move his full body made. "I can get you four. Three hundred thousand each. Cash. Upfront."

"I'm not going to let you take my money and not give me any goods. So, I'll see the women when it's time to exchange, and you'll get your money when I take the girls."

"I don't think so."

Creed sat as still as a rock, staring at Compton, but he didn't say a thing.

Finally, Compton said, "Are we finished?"

"I guess so." Creed stood and moved aside to push his chair in. Compton studied his movements. Creed turned and walked toward the door.

"Wait."

He turned back to Compton but said nothing.

"How do I know you have the money?"

He shrugged. "How do I know you have the girls?"

A long silence spread between them, and Compton laughed. "Touché."

Compton sat back in his chair, "Come back and sit down."

Creed glanced at the chair he'd vacated then at Compton.

"I'm not going to waste my time here. You either want to make a deal or you don't. I have a line on another supplier and am meeting with him tomorrow, so you either want to make a deal or you don't. Either way, I'll get what I want."

"Who is this other supplier you have?"

"I have no intention of telling you that. Other than to say I have a flight booked to Vegas tomorrow morning. You can either make a deal right now, or I'll make one there. You aren't the only game in town."

"Fuck you. I have the best quality. No one can match that."

Creed stared at him and didn't move. Compton's eyes darted back and forth, then he inhaled deeply and sat back in his seat.

"I'm willing to do this. I'm willing to let you see the girls at the money exchange. Bronwyn must have lied to you about how things are done."

"On the contrary. He told me you screwed him over and didn't have younger girls but still charged full price. I'm not going to let that happen to me. I'll see the goods before I pay you a cent. If they are quality and young, you have a deal. If not, I walk."

"You fucker. Who do you fucking think you are?"

"I'm the man with the money."

Compton pulled a small metal box from his breast pocket and took a small pill from inside. He lay it on his tongue and swallowed it without water.

"I'll send you an address in the morning."

"Not going to work. I told you I have a flight booked in the morning."

"You're still going?"

"Oh, absolutely I'm still going."

Compton leaned forward and picked his phone off the table. He tapped a couple of times and held it to his ear.

"Merchi Sorenson wants to see them. One hour."

Without saying goodbye he jabbed at the phone and set it on the table.

"The Old District Warehouses on the river. Warehouse ten eighty. One hour. Bring one point two million in cash. Have transport ready to take them with you."

"Alright. I'll see you there."

Compton sat forward and slapped his hand on the table. "You bring police with you and you'll be dead before they will. I guarantee it."

Creed stood and leaned over the table. He was within four inches from Compton's face. "You fuck me over and you'll be the first one dead. I guarantee it."

They stared at each other for long enough that each was reluctant to look away first. But, in this instance, Compton did. He grabbed his phone from the tabletop and stood. He turned and walked toward the back door and Creed turned and made his way to the front door. He resisted the urge to turn around and see if Compton was pulling a gun on him, and he knew police wouldn't arrest him now because they'd wait until they were at the warehouse.

Exiting the Filibuster, Creed stifled a grin, and Charly walked behind him, neither saying a word. As they rounded the corner Falcon spoke into their comm units.

"Police are on their way to the warehouse to set up. Wade is having him followed to see if he's going there first and what he's doing."

Creed nodded then glanced over at Charly who had a big smile on her face.

ope listened as Creed did his job. Her parents sat with her, Kori, Emmy, and Caiden at the table in the dining room. Even Carmella joined them to listen, her hand usually over her mouth as she heard the discussion.

Once Creed, Charly, Falcon, Diego, and Van were in the SUV and driving back Caiden put their comm units on his computer speaker.

"Nice job, Creed. Nice job."

"Thank you."

He was humble and Emmy smiled.

"Falcon, nice job taking care of Merchi Sorenson."

"Thanks. I didn't have much to do. Diego had him wrapped up before I had to land a punch."

Kori spoke, "I'm glad you didn't have to throw a punch."

"Babe, I so wanted to deck that son of a bitch. He deserves it. He's a trafficker."

Kori nodded. "True. Maybe you can go to the jail and punch him there."

Falcon laughed and so did everyone around the table.

Creed spoke again, "Emmy, we'll need a van to pick up the girls."

"I've already spoken to Wade about it. He'll have one at the ready for us."

Kori looked at Emmy. "You'll need water and meal bars and blankets for them right away. They are usually starving and dehydrated."

Emmy smiled. "Thanks Kori. I'll let Wade know that."

"I'd like to be in the van."

Falcon said. "No. Kori."

"Falcon, I'm an EMT. If any of them need medical assistance, I'll be there."

"Dammit Kori, we've talked about this."

"You just put yourself in a dangerous situation."

Emmy held her hands up. "You two chat about this when you get back. For right now, I'll contact Wade about the supplies for the girls. You five get to the warehouse and sit back. When you see Compton arrive, you go and see the girls. Exchange the money and Wade's men will swoop in. He has a team of eight marines, they'll be dressed in tactical gear but hidden from view until it's time to arrest Compton."

Hope swallowed. "What about his wife, Helen? Will she be arrested?"

Emmy nodded, "Yes. Wade just texted and told me she just left the congressional building."

Hope cocked her head to the side. "Why would she be there when she knew Will wasn't there?"

Emmy's brows rose and she shrugged. "I don't know. I'm not sure we'll be able to find out before we pick her up. She's being driven in a limo and Wade's men are following her. She'll be arrested before she gets home. They'll lock her up in traffic."

"That's brilliant." Hope glanced at her parents who sat watching all of them. She smiled then turned to Emmy. "I want to be there when they arrest him. I want him to see it was me. I want him to think about what he did to me while he sits in jail."

Creed's voice came over the speaker. "Hope, please don't. We don't know who else will be there. For all we know, he'll have men there to ambush us. We just don't know."

"I'll stay in the vehicle until he's arrested. I'll stay hidden, but I want him to know. I want to look him in the eye with his handcuffs on and know it was me."

Creed cleared his throat, "I understand Hope. I do. You'll get your chance, but this isn't a secure place. We don't even know what we're walking into right now. Until we have that area secure, it's dangerous."

"You said Wade would have eight men in tactical gear to help you. How on earth could it be dangerous for me?"

Emmy responded. "Because of the unknown. Right now, we're in the dark."

"You mean like I was while I was tied to a bar on the wall?"

Her mother began crying and one look at her father showed his eyes welled with unshed tears.

"I'm sorry Mom and Dad. I am. But, if I'm to heal, to be whole again, I have to do this. What he did to me and intended to do to me was heinous. No one should ever have to go through that. And, I didn't have it as bad as many others did."

Creed cleared his throat lightly. "Emmy. Can you get Hope here? At the warehouse? If she promises to stay in the SUV until we have Compton and the area secure, that is. She's right. I don't want to take away the chance for her to see that monster arrested. It's something she needs for her mental wellbeing so she can heal. I agree with her on that."

Hope's eyes watered and her breathing changed to short bursts of air instead of deep steady breaths. She swallowed the huge lump that formed in her throat, and she glanced at her parents. "I need this. Please support me in this."

Her father reached across the table and she laid her left hand in his. His fingers squeezed her tightly as his watery eyes stared into hers.

"Please promise to do as they ask and stay safe. We just can't lose you after getting you back."

"I prom..." She halted as a sob rose up in her throat. Taking a deep breath she let it out then started again. "I promise. I love you."

Her mom reached across the table and Hope held each of her parents' hands in hers as Creed's voice called out over Emmy's computer.

"Emmy, text me the details once you have them worked out. We just arrived at the warehouse and we're going to do some recon."

39

When he heard the emotion in her voice and the deep need to see Compton in cuffs, he knew she was right. In order for Hope to have closure and feel safe again and to show that asshole she'd won, she'd need to face him. It would do more for her healing than anything he or anyone else could do. He'd give her this. Hopefully it wasn't a mistake.

Falcon parked the SUV alongside a building several blocks into the warehouse district. Most of the warehouses looked in need of repair. Most looked as though they'd been empty for years. The waterfront used to be the hub of all things coming and going via boat. The warehouses eased the burden on having semis or trucks available to unload cargo. Little was transported via boat in this area anymore, and the need for the waterfront warehouses diminished too. Therefore, it left these buildings to the seedier side of the human element. Enter Compton and humans like him.

Then he had a thought. "Emmy?"

"Go ahead Creed."

"Can you or Caiden run a search to see how many of the buildings down here Compton owns?"

"Sure. What's your purpose?"

"What if he has other buildings and other women in them? Once we arrest him, police should be able to obtain a search warrant and we may just get lucky."

"That's a great point, Creed. I'll see what I can find and I'll have Caiden run a deep search into any companies Compton owns as well. One or more of the companies may also have ownership in a building or two."

"Thanks."

The weather was warm, the sun shone brightly and Creed knew he'd be sweating his ass off in this suit. He pulled the jacket off and Charly shook her head.

"You have to wear that so we can hear you."

"I know, but for right now, until I meet with Compton, I need to stay cool or I'll melt."

"Okay. But keep it close."

"Yes, boss."

Charly shook her head and they each exited the SUV. He glanced around the area and noted the buildings were in a row, and very similar in style and shape, which hopefully meant the insides were close to identical.

Tires crunching on gravel had him jumping back from view and a quick glance showed his team doing the same.

Falcon tapped his comm unit and they each turned theirs back on.

"I'll walk up to the north and see what else is up there. I have this sickening feeling in my stomach Compton is going to have men planted around this area."

Diego nodded. "I have that same feeling. I'll walk to the west and see what I can find."

Creed looked at his teammates and cocked his head to the right. "I'll head east and see what I can find."

Another set of tires crunched on the gravel under its tires. The area looked as though at one time it had been paved but had since broken up and been left unattended. He saw a vehicle, and watched it move on toward the water's edge.

"Vehicle en route to the water's edge."

"Roger." Falcon responded.

Creed edged his way along the buildings, noting the silence that met him other than the occasional airplane overhead or vehicle moving.

He spotted a man ducking between two warehouses up ahead and to his right and called to Emmy.

"Em, are Wade's men here?"

"Checking."

After a few minutes she responded. "Not yet. They are en route."

"Okay. Compton has men here. I see one up ahead and to my right, tucking in behind a building."

Van inched close to Creed and he pointed to where the man stood, rifle at the ready, looking toward the waterfront. "They're going to ambush us."

"Or they're worried we're bringing cops or trying to stiff them on the deal."

Charly neared them and whispered, "There's another man two buildings up to the west."

Creed took a deep breath. "The most they could have had in that vehicle is six men. So, we should assume there are six of them." He looked at his watch. "We have twenty minutes before we're due to the warehouse with Compton. Let's see if we can locate the other men. At the very least, we can give Wade a heads-up."

"Agreed." Charly said before disappearing around the corner.

Falcon went in the opposite direction of Charly and Creed and decided to make his way between the buildings and move forward toward the men they knew were in place. With a little luck, he'd see more of them.

Softly moving along the side of the building, he ducked in wherever there was a nook or cranny, in case the men could hear him. Charly's voice whispered over the comm unit.

"Connor Fitzjarrell just drove toward the waterfront in his Caddy."

Creed nodded. "I bet he's the bodyguard. Sent in to intimidate me."

Emmy then responded. "Wade's men are pulling into the warehouse district now. I informed Wade you've seen others."

"Roger. We just saw Fitzjarrell drive in."

"Roger. Relayed."

Creed inched his way back toward the vehicle and once out of ear shot of anyone close he whispered, "I'm at the SUV. We should prepare to meet Compton."

His shoes made more noise than he liked. He normally wore tactical boots and they were soundless. But the need to dress the part took priority. As soon as he felt comfortable, he turned toward the vehicle, keeping his back against the wall. The feeling that someone was watching began weighing heavy in his chest but he reminded himself not to be paranoid.

The SUV was in sight when he heard tires on the pavement once again. Glancing down the row he noted a large van type vehicle painted flat black driving toward the waterfront.

Turning left then right to make sure no one was watching, he crossed the road between the buildings and climbed into the SUV.

"I'm in the SUV."

Charly responded first. "I saw you. I'm three steps away."

Falcon opened the driver's door and climbed in. Glancing at Creed he nodded but said nothing. Charly, Diego, and

Van climbed into the SUV and Falcon eased them from their parking spot and headed toward the waterfront and his meeting with Compton.

40

Her stomach twisted tightly as they drove closer to the warehouse and her final showdown with Compton. Trying to remember a time when she enjoyed working for Compton, nothing came to mind. She had been so enamored with her job in the congressional buildings. She had been so excited to feel as though she was making a difference. In truth, the six years she worked there would never add up to the difference she was going to make today. Taking the trash out with this pig would be the most important thing she ever did in her life.

Leaving Washington would be the next most important thing she'd do. It's too nasty here. She'd never feel safe here again. And, she'd never trust anyone here. Even when Compton went to prison, there were likely many people on his payroll. Maybe she'd be able to talk her parents into moving. Her brother, Mitch, was in the service and said he was making a career out of it, so what was there here for them if both she and Mitch were gone?

The man Wade sent to drive Kori and her to the warehouse turned onto a road that seemed to go to a desolate run-down area. She'd never been in this part of town before. She laid her hand over her stomach, hoping the roiling would stop soon. Kori reached over and took her hand, and they locked fingers.

Hope glanced at Kori for reassurance but only saw the same fear she felt. She squeezed Kori's fingers a bit tighter.

The two men in the front were stony silent; the passenger, whose name she never heard, stared straight ahead the entire ride. How did someone sit that still in a moving vehicle?

The vehicle pulled behind a building to the far left of the entire area holding all of the matching warehouse buildings. As soon as he parked the passenger finally moved. He tapped his phone and said, "Unit one in place."

That was it. He then went back to sitting perfectly still. Another large SUV, similar to the one she sat in now, slowly crawled past them and went closer to the waterfront. She watched it until it turned in between buildings further ahead of them and disappeared. Soon thereafter, a voice come on through the speakers, "Unit two in place."

She glanced at Kori to see her watching through the windshield. She looked through the windshield too and saw nothing.

"Unit three in place."

The man in the passenger seat finally turned to her and said, "You'll now hear what's happening through Creed's communication device and that of the other RAPTOR operatives. As soon as they've exchanged money, Units two and three will swoop in and arrest Compton. We will then drive you to his location so you can watch him be arrested."

"I want him to see me too."

The passenger looked at the driver and the driver turned his head to see her. "Those are not our orders."

"That's why I'm here. I want him to see me. To know I escaped his clutches and I turned him in."

"I can't allow that unless Commander Daniels gives the order."

"Ask him."

"Ma'am, we don't ask the commander for orders. He gives them."

"But..."

Kori tugged on her hand and squeezed tighter. Softly she said, "Hey, it's okay. When we know it's safe, we'll get out there."

She looked into Kori's eyes for a long time. Sincerity stared back at her and she finally took a breath and slightly nodded.

Kori pulled her hand up to her heart and wrapped her other hand around their joined hands. She hugged their joined hands and Hope settled slightly. She swallowed to moisten her throat and blinked furiously to keep the tears from filling her eyes.

Creed's voice echoed through the speakers in the vehicle.

"Let's see what you have."

Compton replied. "Let's see the money."

Silence filled the air. Finally, clicking sounds and then Compton said, "I'll count it first."

Creed's voice was firm when he replied. "No, you won't. You can count it after the girls are in my possession. We'll sit right here while you do, but you will not get this money until I see the girls."

Sounds could be heard. Walking on gravel. Clinking of something, she wasn't sure what. An old rickety overhead door opening then Compton's voice yelling into an echoing building. "Bring 'em out."

Silence fell for a long time and she thought she'd throw up if something didn't happen soon. Her stomach tightened then flipped and her fingers shook. She realized then how tightly she was squeezing Kori's hand and she loosened her grip just a bit. Kori didn't say a thing.

The faint sound of crying could be heard and her heartbeat sped up so fast it was as if she were running. Multiple girls crying and footsteps on the gravel.

Creed said, "How old are you?"

"Chetyrnadtsat'."

Kori whispered. "Fourteen."

"How old are you?"

"Pyatnadtsat'."

She looked at Kori. "Fifteen."

Two more times Creed asked for ages and was told, fourteen.

Silence fell again, then Compton's irritated voice spat out. "Are you going to stare all fucking day? Do we have a deal?"

Creed growled, "Yes. We have a deal." Then, to Hope's surprise, in perfect Russian, Creed said, "Pereyti k furgonu."

Hope turned to Kori, her brows furrowed. "I don't know."

The driver softly translated, "Go to the van."

Footsteps on gravel sounded lightly and Compton spat out, "You owe me one point two million dollars, Sorenson."

"That I do." Creed said. "It's all there."

In a flash, yelling began and shots rang out. The melee that ensued seemed chaotic and horrible to listen to. She didn't hear Creed speak anymore and she began crying. Kori sobbed next to her, and Hope leaned over to wrap an arm around Kori's shoulders. "He's okay. They both are."

The sounds stopped and the driver started the SUV.

Hope sat up straight to watch the direction they headed and the instant he turned the corner near the front row of buildings Hope's heart pounded so hard in her chest she thought she'd pass out.

41

Creed caught his breath then turned to check on his teammates. Falcon stood a few feet from him, Connor Fitzjarrell laid on the ground at his feet. Falcon breathed heavily, his eyes still a bit wild after that commotion.

Turning to his right, he saw Charly kneeling down checking the pulse of a man on the ground. She stood and caught his gaze, then shook her head.

Van stood over a man lying on the ground unmoving and Diego finished zip tying the wrists of a man on the ground.

He heard the vehicle approach and spun around as it came to a stop alongside the crying girls who'd huddled together behind his SUV when the shooting started.

Not moving an inch, he waited to see who was inside, friend or foe? His gun still in his hand. When the door opened and a man in tactical clothing stepped out, then the back door swung open and Hope jumped out and ran to him, his heart did a different dance.

He holstered his gun, stepped away from Compton and caught Hope as she lunged and wrapped her in his arms. She felt like a favorite blanket wrapped around him. Warm, soft, and safe. She smelled like a fresh spring morning and he never wanted to feel or smell anything other than Hope again.

She wept quietly into his neck and he held her until she calmed. His heart finally began to return to its normal rhythm and he closed his eyes and held Hope.

"Sir."

He lifted his head and looked at the men who stood before him. "I'm sorry she got out of the vehicle. I didn't know she'd do that."

Creed chuckled. "It's fine. I've got her."

He lowered Hope to the ground and looked into her eyes. "Compton's been shot, but he isn't dead. But, two of his men are. Fitzjarrell and I don't have ID on the other one yet."

"Okay." She swallowed. "Is he conscious?"

Creed shrugged. He turned his body and wrapped his arm around her shoulders. Ushering her the few steps to where Compton lay, he watched as she looked down at him.

"Wake up you piece of shit." She kicked him in the side. Not hard enough to do damage, just hard enough that he felt it for certain.

His eyes opened and she leaned down and looked him directly in the eyes. "You see me asshole?" Hope stood a bit taller. "You see me? I'm here. I escaped. And I brought you down. You're going to prison where you'll be raped every day for the rest of your life. I want you to think of me and all the other women you've hurt every time you're attacked in prison."

Compton's dead eyes stared back at her. He finally said, "Fuck you, whore."

He was ready to grab Hope if she tried to kill him, but she looked at him and started laughing. Her laughter grew and she held her hand over her tummy as she laughed.

She turned to him and he liked seeing her like this. Her face wasn't tight with fear or anger, her eyes danced and her smile was brilliant.

"Can we go home now?"

He kissed her lips. "We can soon. I'll have to wait for the police to arrest Compton and give a statement. Wade's men will take Compton into custody then we can leave."

Emmy spoke to him through his comm unit. "Great job team. Fantastic. Helen Compton has just been arrested and is on her way to the base."

Compton laughed, then coughed. "I'll be out of jail in an hour."

Creed turned to him. "Actually you won't. We have enough evidence to keep you in prison for the rest of your life."

"My wife will have me bailed out in an hour."

Creed smiled. "Your wife has been arrested and is in custody and neither of you will be getting out of anywhere. You won't even be held in a regular jail cell because we know how corrupt this town is. The military has agreed to hold you until trial."

"You don't have the right to do that."

"Actually, I do."

Two of Wade's men exited the building Compton had the girls in and shook their heads no. At least there weren't any others. Not in this building anyway. He'd find out later if Compton owned other warehouses.

Sirens approached and Creed looked over to see Kori and Falcon helping the girls Compton had held as hostage. Kori wrapped each of them in a blanket and both she and Falcon opened bottles of water and handed out meal bars. He smiled as his friend assisted others with his new bride.

Charly walked over to the girls and sat down next to one of them and spoke softly to her. The police car stopped before the mess they'd made around the front of the warehouse and Wade's men approached them and filled them in on what happened. Creed nodded at them as they walked past him and toward the bodies lying on the ground. More sirens approached and an ambulance turned the corner and halted behind the police cars.

He and Hope quietly watched as the EMTs pulled a stretcher out and ran to Compton.

One of Wade's men approached them and nodded. "Sir. We're to bring you all in to the base to speak with

Commander Daniels. He needs a debrief immediately and he'll need to get your statements."

"Understood. What will happen to the girls?"

The man looked at the girls huddled together on the ground, eating and drinking water as if they hadn't eaten in days. "We'll take them with us as well and they'll be checked over by medical staff and taken care of until we can send them home."

Creed nodded and looked down at Hope who stood still and silent next to him. She looked up at him and smiled. Then she asked, "When can we go into the congressional building and get my evidence?"

"We'll talk to Emmy about that after we've finished with Commander Daniels."

"Who is Commander Daniels?"

Creed smiled. "Wade. Wade Daniels."

"He's a commander?"

Creed laughed. "He's so much more than that. I'll explain later."

42

Hope woke when the vehicle slowed. She lay tucked into Creed's side, warm and safe where she'd promptly fallen fast asleep.

"Okay sleepyhead, we're home."

She sat straight and looked through the windshield at the inside of the garage and yawned. Charly turned back to her from the passenger seat, "You okay?"

"Yeah. I'm just not used to shootouts and rescues I guess."

Charly laughed and so did Creed and the others. He opened the door and slid out of the vehicle, waiting for her to scoot over and out. Kori sat on the other side of her and Falcon already had her door open and pulled into his arms. Van and Diego exited from the back of the vehicle and they began walking toward the Bowman home.

The back door of the house flew open and her mom and dad ran toward them. She met them in the middle and hugged both of her parents to her.

"I'm so happy to see you're alright. We were listening, but then the shooting..." Her mom broke into a sob and Hope hugged her once again.

She glanced at her father's watery eyes and closed hers so she didn't burst into tears.

Creed's hand lay at the small of her back. "Let's go inside and debrief."

Hope nestled herself into his side and she and Creed followed her parents into the kitchen of the Bowman home.

Sighing heavily upon entering the kitchen, her knees began shaking. She wrapped her arm tightly around Creed.

His brows furrowed. "Are you alright?"

"Yes." She whispered, "I think it's all catching up to me now though."

"Okay. Let's go sit in the living room."

Her mother turned and concern filled her face. Hope shook her head. "I'm alright mom. I think I just got an adrenaline rush."

Creed got her safely to the sofa. "What do you need? Water or tea?"

"Tea would be wonderful."

Creed left the room and her mom sat next to her. Emmy entered the room along with everyone else.

Emmy sat in the chair directly to her left. "Hope, are you alright with us debriefing?"

"Yes, of course."

Emmy set her laptop on her lap and opened the lid. Creed entered the room with her tea and her mom promptly scooted over for him to sit next to her. That was something.

Emmy started the debrief. "Thank you all for the amazing work you did today. Here's how things have shaped since the congressman's arrest. He's being held in a separate cell from his wife on base. Commander Daniels managed to get the CIA involved since the trafficking takes place across state and country borders. That is a boon to us and our mission. With the help of Commander Daniels and the CIA, we've secured permission to enter the congressional building tomorrow at eight o'clock a.m. They are locking the building to anyone else trying to get in and we'll be the only people on the premises. We can only enter with a CIA escort."

Creed looked at her and smiled. "We'll grab your evidence tomorrow."

She rested her hand on her tummy. "Oh my God, that is fantastic."

Emmy smiled. "Together with the names and phone numbers you had previously given us, the CIA has tracked down four of the fifteen names and they are continuing to track down the others."

Emmy tapped on her computer a few times and Hope noticed how everyone sat still and quiet waiting for her to continue the debrief.

"The CIA is in the Compton home right now doing a thorough search." Emmy then looked directly at her. "Hope, they are asking if there are certain things they should pay close attention to locating."

"Yes. Compton always used burner phones. He had a few of them. One was a dark blue flip phone. One was a black flip phone, and one was a lighter blue flip phone. Sometimes he'd toss them in the top right drawer of his desk, but he usually put them in his briefcase and took them home."

Hope took a deep breath. "That reminds me. Did the CIA search the vehicle Compton rode to the warehouse in? He may have those phones and his briefcase in that vehicle. It's doubtful he'd leave it anywhere to be found unless they were left at his house. But if he was meeting to make a deal, he'd likely have those with him."

"Let me ask." Emmy typed out a message and sent it, then continued. "Merchi Sorenson is also in a cell on base. He's talking, though not without asking for something in return. And, he told the CIA he has access to Anton Smith. Hope, are you aware of Sorenson and Smith having any type of relationship?"

"No. I'd never heard of him until you mentioned his name."

"Okay. They're asking him for proof that he even knows Smith or how to reach him."

Emmy looked up at her and smiled. "Thank you so much for all of the help you've given us Hope. Getting these traffickers off the streets is our number one priority and why we were formed."

Creed wrapped his arm around her and squeezed and she felt her cheeks heat. "Thank you for saving me. Without you all, I..." She swallowed the emotion clogging her throat. "I don't know where I'd be or if I'd even be alive."

Creed kissed the top of her head, and she heard her mom sniff. She didn't want to be morose, she wanted to celebrate that they were getting close, and the Comptons wouldn't be able to do this to anyone else.

"Can you ask the CIA to pick up Justin at Byte Me? If they question him, they may be able to tie him to calling Compton and Compton having everything to do with my kidnapping."

Emmy smiled at her. "They have him in custody now."

Creed leaned forward and rested his forearms on his knees. "During our debrief with the CIA, I mentioned the six men we saw watching us. They said they couldn't tell me anything at that time. Have you been given an update on it?"

Emmy looked at her computer and scrolled. "Not yet. Is there something specific you noticed?"

He looked back at her and his lips frowned slightly. "Hope told me one of the men who took her had a limp. That was the man at the hospital, but one of the men I saw today also had a limp. She remembered as they carried her from her apartment."

He looked at her again and she stared at him. He'd remembered that small detail that she'd told him during one of their late-night chats. She still woke at three a.m., and he still sat and talked with her until she calmed.

43

H e exited the bathroom and softly crossed the floor to the bed where Hope lay on her side, her head in her hand, watching him. She was a sight to behold for sure. He wanted her. The way she looked at him right now excited him.

She pulled the covers back and patted the empty spot next to her with a sexy smile on her face.

He accepted the invitation eagerly.

The instant he lay back, she rose up and kissed his lips. Her left hand cupped the back of his head and she turned hers to fit their lips together perfectly. His body roared to life.

Hope tugged at the sweatpants he wore and he eagerly helped her slip them down his hips and he tossed them to the floor. She wore a tiny satin cami top and as he reached down to feel her, no panties. Nice.

His fingers felt her flesh as it heated, then slipped further down her body and sought the fine curls between her legs. Rolling his fingers over her warm, soft flesh, he slid further between her legs until he felt her wetness. Dipping his finger inside her easily, he pulled out and wet her clit, which she enjoyed.

Her lips pulled from his and he watched her beautiful face as it rose over him, and wrapped her hand around his cock. Slowly massaging him, up and down, he swallowed to moisten his throat and arch his hips up to meet her movements. Slowly, she rose up, placed his cock at her entrance and slowly slid down onto him in the most sensual movement he'd ever experienced. The tiny "o" that formed her lips was erotic, the look in her eyes as she rose and fell on him repeatedly enthralled him.

His hands were on her hips and he helped her pump up and down as their skin heated and his heart pounded in his chest. He was torn between watching her and closing his eyes to feel it all. Which was better? It was an impossible decision. He opted for both. He closed his eyes for a bit, then opened them to watch the emotions play on her face as she rose and fell on him.

She gasped lightly, then put her hand over her mouth so as not to make noise. She sped up and placed her hand on his chest, biting her bottom lip as she let her orgasm roll over her. A more beautiful sight he'd never seen.

He rolled her over quickly and pumped into her a few times, letting the fire that raged from deep within his balls spew out of him with a burst of pain and pleasure so intense he marveled at how he didn't combust.

Once he'd gotten his breathing under control, he rolled over and pulled tissues from the box on the bedside table.

Hope kissed his lips, then strode into the bathroom, only the very bottom of her cute butt exposed for his view.

When she exited the bathroom a couple minutes later, she smiled brightly at him, kissed his lips once more and nestled into his side until they both fell fast asleep.

Creed woke to the sounds of birds chirping loudly and voices below chatting. He looked at his watch and saw that it was just after six. Looking to his right, Hope lay peacefully asleep, her dark hair fanned out over the pillow, her cute little satin cami slightly askew and a rosy, pink nipple greeting him a good day.

He leaned over and kissed her nipple which woke her enough that her left hand caressed his hair.

"Morning."

He chuckled. "Morning."

She stretched, "What time is it?"

"Just after six."

Her eyes flew open. "Really?"

"Yes. Really."

Hope sat up and looked around the room as if for the first time. Turning her head to look at him she smiled. "I didn't wake at three in the morning."

He sat up and examined her face then kissed her lips. "I guess you'll have to work up a good sweat every night before bed. Life is looking up."

She giggled and gently punched his arm. "Be serious."

He nibbled her ear. "Oh, baby, I am serious."

He kissed her jaw, her neck, then her shoulder. "We have to get ready to head to the congressional building. And I think I smell coffee."

"Okay. Is it okay if I'm nervous?"

"Of course it's okay. You haven't been there since just before you were taken. And you know all the nasty stuff that goes on in that building, so it's natural you'd be nervous." He scooted off the side of the bed and picked up the sweatpants he'd haphazardly discarded last night and pulled his prosthetic from its resting spot alongside the bed. "But, this time, we'll all be there with you and the CIA won't let anyone inside while we're there."

"But people will know something is going on."

"Yes, Emmy said last night that the CIA is going to call it a bomb threat. We'll go in the back and into the underground parking garage and hopefully slip out somewhat undetected."

"What do you mean somewhat?"

"There's always a reporter or some blogger looking to crack a hot case. Especially in Washington, so it's doubtful even the CIA can stop everyone from lurking about. But, you'll be protected."

"Okay." She scooted off the bed on her side. "Why don't you take your shower first? I want to check my notes before we go so I remember every little detail."

"Okay." He leaned down and kissed her lips before opening his dresser drawer, pulling out clean clothes for today. His drawers were full which told him Carmella had stealthily done laundry while they were out. He chuckled as he went into the bathroom to clean up for the day.

44

Hope practiced her calming breathing that Charly had shown her. Breathe in deep for the count of ten. Breathe out for the count of ten. It seemed to help, as much as it could. Her nerves had been on a rollercoaster today. It started with Carmella looking hurt that she couldn't eat breakfast. Once she assured Carmella it had nothing to do with the food and everything to do with her nerves, Carmella packed a to-go container and insisted she take it.

"You never know, Ms. Hope."

The crowds that had gathered around the congressional buildings to rubberneck the situation were larger than the inauguration. It was crazy that people would come toward a bomb threat, rather than run away. Cell phones were out and recording everything and Hope sat back in her seat, nestled between Creed and Charly. Falcon drove and Emmy was in the passenger seat, Diego, Van, and Caiden followed in the second SUV.

The guards waved them in, and right this minute they were driving down a long drive into the underground parking garage. There were a few cars parked in the garage, which was normal, but she thought they had evacuated the building.

Creed nudged her. "It's likely the owners of these vehicles weren't allowed to come down and get their cars before evacuation."

She smiled weakly and nodded but she stared into his beautiful brown eyes because it made her feel better.

Falcon parked the SUV and called out. "Ready?"

"Yeah." She said weakly then decided she didn't like sounding weak, so she pulled her shoulders back and decided she'd go in there and get the evidence needed to put the Comptons away and she was strong enough to do it.

Creed exited to her right, and she followed him from the vehicle. He took her hand, and they walked as a group to the elevator. A CIA agent nodded to them as they approached, and Emmy showed him her ID and introduced the group of them. The agent then nodded, "My name is Cooper. Agent Cooper."

He opened the elevator for them and they stepped inside. During the ride up, she practiced her breathing but kept her shoulders high and her back strong. She could do this. She'd been through hell this past month, but things were looking up. Definitely up.

When the doors opened, she exited with the group. They were joined by another CIA agent who said his name was

Brown. She wondered if they got to pick their own names. As they walked down the massive hall of doors, leading to the congressmen and women's outer offices then their inner sanctums. It had taken her a while to remember which was Compton's door when she'd first started. She'd counted the doors to keep herself straight and she remembered a day she'd lost count and had to start over.

She stopped at the door to her former office and took a giant breath. Creed squeezed her hand, and she looked up into his eyes and smiled. "I'm ready."

He grinned and they proceeded into the office.

She looked around at the furnishings, still the same as the last day she'd been here. Only now, her desk was piled with folders and papers. Whoever they'd replaced her with needed some assistance and that made her smile. She never left her desk a mess. It was a source of pride for her.

"Hope." She looked at Creed. "Tell us where to begin."

She swallowed and looked at the large floor to ceiling bookcase behind her desk. "It's up there."

She pointed to a shelf second from the ceiling. "I needed a ladder to get up there, so I called maintenance to come and fix a bulb." She pointed above them. "I told them it buzzed."

Creed grinned at her. "When maintenance left to get another bulb, I used the ladder and climbed up there. It's the third book from the wall. The title is *The Underground Railroad*."

Emmy turned to her and grinned. "Subtle."

Creed looked up at the shelves. "How often are those dusted?"

"Not often. I had to be careful when I pulled the book out not to disturb anything."

A man entered the room with a ladder and Hope shook her head. She hadn't heard anyone call for it. She started toward the ladder when Creed held her arm. "They have to do it." He pointed to the CIA.

She nodded and waited as one of the agents climbed the ladder. He pulled the book from the shelf and started down the ladder.

"Wait." Hope called.

The agent stopped.

"I also tossed a thumb drive behind the books. It's a different one than the one I took to Byte Me."

The agent pulled the books from the shelves and found a thumb drive behind. He held it up and began descending the ladder. Hope walked to the edge of her desk where the agent laid the book. He nodded at her. "Go ahead and show me."

Her fingers shook as she opened the book. "I had to be careful not to crease the spine or it might show use." She lifted the cover carefully and flipped to the middle of the book where she'd hollowed out a small space and pulled three folded sheets of paper and a thumb drive from inside.

She shakily handed them to the agent. "There are names, dates, dollar amounts, banks, and locations where

Compton was meeting them. The thumb drive is the recordings of those conversations. The thumb drive that I gave Emmy has more of the same."

The CIA agent finally smiled. "This is very good Ms. Dumond."

She swallowed and turned to smile at Creed. His smile in return was breathtaking.

The agent she'd given the papers to, took a picture of the papers she'd given him, then looked at his agents as he sent a text. "Okay, search for anything that has these names, phone numbers, banks, or any travel plans." He turned back to her. "Ms. Dumond, do you know where the congressman kept his travel itinerary?"

She nodded. "I'd have to log into the system. If they haven't wiped my information out that is."

He shrugged. "Give it a shot."

She sat at her former desk and though her fingers shook, she managed to log into her computer and her heart raced. "They didn't erase me."

Creed came to stand by her. "Likely didn't think you'd be back to be a threat."

"Yeah." She showed the agent, "These are the files. But he hid his personal travel itineraries in here." She clicked another folder then another one and opened up pages of personal travel.

The agent nodded, "Thank you Ms. Dumond. Please step aside as we download what we need. We'll then take the computer to the lab for further forensic investigation."

Another agent replaced her in her chair and his fingers sped over the keys with ease. She walked to Creed and stood next to him. His arm wrapped around her shoulders and pulled her into his body, and she was grateful for the support. Her knees still shook.

45

They sat at the dining room table for their final debrief here in Washington DC. Emmy was in the office on the telephone with the CIA and Commander Daniels, and they eagerly waited for her news.

Charly poured fresh coffee for those drinking it then sat down. "I'm excited to get home and see what Sam got for me."

Falcon chuckled. "He gets you something every time you go on a mission. You're spoiled."

"So?"

Kori laughed. "I think that's really sweet of him."

Hope sat quietly next to him. Her parents were still upstairs packing to leave.

Emmy entered the room, "Okay. Here's what happened."

She sat at the head of the table, lay her phone on top and took a deep breath. "Wade...Commander Daniels and the CIA believe Smith is in the Ozarks, based on the information they've gathered from the men they have at the base. A small town just outside of Jasper. I've convinced them, at least for now, to let us finish this mission. They're giving us two weeks. Then they're taking over. I know you all feel the same as I do. I want to wrap this mission up. I want RAPTOR to finish what we started. Tell me your thoughts."

He answered first. "Yes. We need to finish this."

Falcon replied as well. "Absolutely. This is ours."

Charly nodded. "Same."

Van sat forward and heaved out a deep breath. "There's no question."

Diego nodded. "We absolutely want this finished on our watch."

Caiden sat quietly, his fingers running over his keyboard. "I think we all need and deserve this."

"So, this is what I think we need to do. Diego, Van, Caiden, and Charly, we should go to the Ozarks and finish this. Falcon and Creed, you've both been out for a while, you can go home if you'd prefer."

Creed shook his head. "No. I'm in on this."

Falcon looked at Kori and she nodded. "We're in on this one too."

Emmy looked at Kori. "Kori, are you sure?"

"I'm an EMT. I can help. And I want to see this through as much as you. It's just as personal to me, maybe in a different way, but still personal."

Emmy nodded. "Charly? You can go home and help from there. There will be plenty to do. Cyber will be working overtime to pull all the intel we need. To be honest, I'd love it if you'd help with that. But, if you absolutely want to come to the Ozarks, I understand."

Charly swallowed. "I'll go where you need me, Emmy. More than anything, what's important is that we capture Smith and I'd love to be there when we do."

"Caiden, I'd like you to go home and work with Cyber on gathering and organizing the intel we have. Commander Daniels will give you clearance to the information they have and will gather as they continue to question those they have in custody."

"Whatever you need Em."

Emmy inhaled a deep breath. "Let me think on this a bit. Therese will be here at two this afternoon. In the meantime, finish your reports and get ready to board."

Falcon and Kori stood and left the room. Charly left right behind them. He looked down at Hope and quietly said, "Let's go have a chat."

The solemn look she gave him nearly gutted him. But she quietly stood and started walking to the doorway. He stood but Emmy stopped him. Quietly she said, "Do you have a plan?"

"I do. I'm going to share it with Hope right now. I'll fill you in later."

Emmy nodded and Creed caught up to Hope. He took her hand as they ascended the grand staircase, his gut was twisted and tight. He opened the door to their room and pulled her into it before closing the door quietly.

Hope turned, her eyes wet and glistening. "Are you breaking up with me?"

He swallowed. "No." He took her hand again and pulled her to the bed. He sat on the edge and tugged her to sit beside him.

"Hope. I know this is unusual. How we got together is anything but normal. But we've spent practically every hour of every day together these past weeks and I don't want to stop. You can't stay here in DC. I don't think you'll ever feel safe here. And, it's filled with vermin. Come back to Lynyrd Station with me. Let's see where we go. Your parents can come too. We'll help them find a place to live and you'll be so surprised at how nice it is." He cleared his throat. "I'm not very eloquent here."

He turned to face her and laid his hand along her jaw. "I love you Hope. I can honestly say I've never been head over heels in love with anyone before in my life. But...My God, I'm in love with you."

Tears streamed down her cheeks, and she daintily sniffed. He reached over and pulled a tissue from the box on the table and handed it to her. She dabbed at her eyes and nose, then took a deep breath and looked into his eyes. His stomach was still a tightly wound ball of twine.

"Creed." She chuckled and shook her head. "I thought you were going to break up with me, so give me a minute to get my head around the fact that you didn't."

She dabbed her nose once again. She looked deeply into his eyes and lay her hand along his jaw. Leaning in she kissed his lips softly. "I love you, Creed Rowan. I was worried I was a cliché. Falling in love with her protector. But, I did fall in love with you and you are so much more to me than that. We've sat up in the middle of the night and talked about everything and nothing. You've held my hand through the darkest moments of my life. You're a badass, sexy monster of a man and I love every inch of you."

His arms wrapped her into a tight embrace, and he laid back on the bed and squeezed her tighter to him. He inhaled the scent of her hair and her skin and the feel of how she fit into his body. "I never want to let you go."

She giggled. "Good. I never want you to."

After they'd cried and hugged and laughed, he whispered. "We should go talk to your parents."

"Yeah."

He squeezed her once again then sat up and pulled her up with him. Taking her hand in his he led her to the door and just as they stepped into the hall, her parents were leaving their room.

"Mom and Dad, can we talk to you for a few minutes?"

Her parents looked at each other, then at him, and he wasn't sure what the look they landed on him meant, but he was about to find out.

They went into her parents' room, and the Dumonds sat on their bed while he and Hope took the chairs facing the fireplace. Creed turned the chairs around to face them and waited for Hope to sit.

He looked at Hope, then to her parents. "Today at two our pilot, Therese, will be here to take us home. Actually..." He stopped and looked at Hope, his brows high on his forehead. "I forgot to ask if you're coming to the Ozarks."

"Of course I am."

He smiled. "Whew."

He shook his head to clear it. "I love Hope. As in, I'm in love with her. She's coming with me. First to the Ozarks to finish this mission, but then to Lynyrd Station where we live. It's a small town in Indiana. We live in a beautiful building we call The Compound, but isn't anything like a compound. We have kids running around all over from our operatives and the GHOST operatives. They're all having babies left and right. Our jobs are dangerous, our home life isn't. We keep it simple, secure, safe, and happy. Hope will always be safe. I pray, she'll always be happy. I'm going to try."

He looked at her and the glorious smile on her face. He felt his cheeks heat and he looked at the Dumonds again. "You're welcome to come with us. I mean, to Lynyrd Station. The Ozarks will be a bit dangerous and chaotic, kind of like it was here. But we've chased this group for a couple of years, and we have to finish bringing them down. We'll help you find a house in Lynyrd Station. You can have cows and horses or dogs or nothing. You can enjoy the fresh country air and the simplicity of life there. Hope will be there and when Mitch comes home, there'll be a place for him either with us or with you, but we'll always welcome him. You'll love my teammates and their spouses and my GHOST teammates, of which you've met Hawk and Roxanne." He held his hands up to encompass the room. "Who are generous, smart, and welcoming."

He leaned over and took Hope's hand and squeezed. Kole cleared his throat. "Does this mean you'll be getting married?"

"Dad!" Hope screeched.

His heart pounded in his chest. "Of course. I mean, I hope so. I mean..." He shook his head and looked at Hope. "I'm sorry, when we chatted, I didn't get that far."

Hope giggled. "We've had a lot to talk about."

Looking Mr. Dumond in the eyes, "I don't have a ring. I haven't had the time. It's been a bit hectic."

Carolyne stood. "Wait." She rummaged through the suitcase lying open on the bed. "Wait. I brought Grandma's ring."

Hope laughed. "You brought jewelry?"

"I didn't know if we'd get to go home again. I didn't know what to do so I grabbed the things I didn't want to lose."

Carolyne pulled the ring from a valet pouch in the corner of her suitcase and held it out to him.

"You can get her a different ring if you want. Or she wants. But this can make it official until then."

The center stone was large, on a narrow white gold band. Simple yet elegant. He looked her in the eyes and nodded as he took the ring from her. Glancing at Kole, he saw the man had tears welling in his eyes. He hoped they were happy tears. Creed nodded at his future father-in-law and turned to Hope. He kissed her ring finger again, then held her grandmother's engagement ring before her, then knelt down on one knee before Hope.

He took her hands in his. "Hope Dumond, will you marry me?"

Her smile was brighter than the sun in the sky. Her eyes stared deeply into his and she squeezed his hands. "Yes. A thousand times yes."

He leaned in for a kiss then slid the ring on her finger. Standing, he pulled her to her feet, wrapped his arms around her, and squeezed her tightly to him and closed his eyes. This was a moment to feel and remember.

When he set her down, he heard her mom sniff and remembered they were there.

"Yes. We're getting married." Pulling Hope's left hand up, he kissed her ring finger. He turned to Hope, "When we're able, I'll get you an engagement ring."

"It's fine Creed. This is a family heirloom and I love it."

"I love you, Hope."

She whispered, "I love you too, Creed."

46

Creed helped Hope from the SUV as her parents climbed from the back seat. Emmy, Falcon, Van, Diego, Charly, and Kori were in the second SUV and Emmy would take the Dumonds back to the Bowman home until Wade's men could escort them to their home. They'd spend the next week preparing their home for sale and organizing the packing up of their belongings. Wade's men would ensure they were protected. Hope was beyond excited when her parents agreed it was time for a major change.

He watched as Hope hugged her mother tightly. Kole approached him with a smile on his face. "I won't tell you how hard it is saying goodbye to her after all we've all been through. But we both feel better knowing you're with her and she'll be protected. I'm counting on you to keep her safe."

Creed held his right hand out to shake Kole's and smiled at his future father-in-law. "I'll protect her with my life."

Kole simply nodded before Hope approached and wrapped her arms around his shoulders. Kole lifted her from the ground and held her tightly as they whispered their goodbyes.

Carolyne stood next to him and sniffed. "Take care of yourselves while in the Ozarks; we want you both to come home safely."

He leaned down and hugged her, for the first time since he'd known them. He squeezed her tightly and whispered, "I'll protect her with my life. I promise you that."

"Keep yourself safe too."

"I promise to do my best. I have excellent teammates."

Carolyne squeezed him tightly then stepped back.

Emmy joined them and Falcon and Kori each waved goodbye to the Dumonds and boarded the plane.

Emmy turned to him. "Creed, when you arrive in the Ozarks, I have an Airbnb set up for us. I've texted you the address. Pick up the two SUVs from the rental agency then spend the first two days going over all the intel we've gathered from interviews as well as what Cyber has pieced together. Helen Compton started talking about three this morning and she's working hard for a deal. Wade will submit his reports by ten tomorrow morning. We're going to get Smith."

Creed chuckled. "Fucking right we are."

"So, rest up, fill your head with our intelligence and I'll see you in two days."

Charly joined them. "Take care of yourself you two." She turned to the Dumonds. "I'll send you every available house I can find and I already have Shelby and Hadleigh watching for them too. When you get to Lynyrd Station, we'll go house-hunting. In the meantime, you can use my old room at the compound."

Carolyne took Charly's hands in hers. "Thank you, Charly. Safe travels to you."

Charly nodded, shook Kole's hand then turned to Hope. "When you and Creed get back home, we'll start planning a wedding."

Hope chuckled and glanced at her mom.

Carolyne wrapped an arm around Charly's shoulders. "We'll have a lot of it planned for you by the time you get home."

"Oh my God, Mom. Slow down."

"Look, who knows if Mitch will settle down. But I've managed to witness my daughter's engagement and I'm so excited to plan the wedding with you."

"You mean for me?"

"No, well, you're busy for the moment, so Charly and I are helping."

"Oh my gawd, I don't even know what to say. Can we just be engaged for a while?"

Charly laughed, "Take all the time you need. Two weeks or so."

Creed pulled Hope to his body and started them toward the plane. "It's time to go."

The Dumonds and Emmy called out their goodbyes and Charly followed them to the plane giggling.

Once they seated themselves on the plane, Falcon glanced across the aisle at him, his phone in hand. "Smith seems to have a family compound in the woods. Looks like we'll be hiking."

Creed laughed. "I haven't been on a good reconnaissance hike in years."

"That's what I was thinking."

Creed pulled his phone out of his pocket and glanced at Hope. "Sorry babe, gotta work."

She chuckled, "No worries, I need a nap anyway."

Creed began reading the reports as they taxied the runway. Charly turned around with her phone in hand. "I think Emmy's going to struggle with this mission. But, she's stubborn."

Kori leaned forward. "I've already called my friend, Chase. He's a doctor and he's in a small hospital outside of Fort Leonard Wood. I think he can help her, so I'm hopeful I'll get them to meet while we're there."

Charly grinned, "I love that. You should be an operative Kori."

Kori held up her hands, "No thanks. I'll leave that to you experts. I'm only here for my husband and medical assistance."

Creed sat back and read the reports as they flew. He couldn't sleep now; this mission was finally nearing the end and his excitement was in overdrive.

Hope moved her hands and he glanced down to see her watching the scenery from the window.

"Can't sleep?"

"No, I thought I could, but I'm struggling to sleep. I'm nervous and excited and, oh, did you hear, I just got engaged."

He chuckled. "We could just sneak off and get married."

"Ugh, my parents would be devastated. Besides, Mom is right, who knows if Mitch will ever settle down. So, they'll need to live vicariously through me for the wedding."

He nodded. "Makes sense." He twisted in his seat so he faced her. "Do you want a big wedding?"

She rolled her head to face him. "Not really. I'd just like it small and nice."

"What about any friends in Washington?"

"No. From what I've managed to figure out, none of them lifted a finger to help find me while I was gone and a couple of them concurred with Compton in the newspaper that I was a drug addict. Those are not friends."

"Truth." He swallowed. "You'll have true friends at home. No one associated with us is dishonest. None of them would sell you out for gain or profit."

Hope swallowed. "I'm looking forward to a life like that. With you." She sat up straighter. "Mostly I'm looking forward to a life with you."

He kissed her fingers. "Me too. Now, we have much more to learn about each other. So, what's your favorite movie?"

"*Dirty Dancing.*"

He hung his head. "Okay. Favorite song?"

"'*Someday I'll be Saturday Night*' by Bon Jovi."

He nodded. "Okay, I can get behind that one, but *Dirty Dancing*? Mehhh." He spread his fingers out and rocked his hand back and forth.

She giggled. "What's your favorite movie?"

"*Die Hard.*"

Her head hit the back of her seat. "Oh no. That's Mitch's favorite movie too."

"I think Mitch and I are going to enjoy some movie time when he comes to visit."

His phone chimed and he looked at the text from Cyber. "We've pinpointed Smith's compound to within a fifty-mile radius. I'm working on narrowing it to twenty miles, but there are cars coming from several directions there."

He turned to Falcon and Van and saw them reading the same text. Falcon turned to him. "We'll narrow that down to right on top of that fucker."

Creed reached his fist out and Falcon bumped it. "Damn straight we will."

. . .

Are you ready for Emmy's story. Grab your copy of Engaging Emersyn and see what happens when she finally meets Chase Nicholas.

Download Engaging Emersyn now!

ALSO BY PJ FIALA

You can find all of my books at https://pjfiala.com/books

Romantic Suspense

Rolling Thunder Series

Moving to Love, Book 1

Moving to Hope, Book 2

Moving to Forever, Book 3

Moving to Desire, Book 4

Moving to You, Book 5

Moving Home, Book 6

Moving On, Book 7

Rolling Thunder Boxset, Books 1-3

Military Romantic Suspense

Second Chances Series

Designing Samantha's Love, Book 1

Securing Kiera's Love, Book 2

Second Chances Boxset - Duet

Bluegrass Security Series

Heart Thief, Book One

Finish Line, Book Two

Lethal Love, Book Three

Wrenched Fate, Book Four

Bluegrass Security Boxset, Books 1-3

Big 3 Security

Ford: Finding His Fire Book One

Lincoln: Finding His Mark Book Two

Dodge: Finding His Jewel Book Three

Rory: Finding His Match Book Four

Big 3 Security Boxset, Books 1-3

GHOST

Defending Keirnan, GHOST Book One

Defending Sophie, GHOST Book Two

Defending Roxanne, GHOST Book Three

Defending Yvette, GHOST Book Four

Defending Bridget, GHOST Book Five

Defending Isabella, GHOST Book Six

RAPTOR

RAPTOR Rising - Prequel

Saving Shelby, RAPTOR Book One

MEET PJ

Writing has been a desire my whole life. Once I found the courage to write, life changed for me in the most profound way. Bringing stories to readers that I'd enjoy reading and creating characters that are flawed, but lovable is such a joy.

When not writing, I'm with my family doing something fun. My husband, Gene, and I are bikers and enjoy riding to new locations, meeting new people and generally enjoying this fabulous country we live in.

I come from a family of veterans. My grandfather, father, brother, two sons, and one daughter-in-law are all veterans. Needless to say, I am proud to be an American and proud of the service my amazing family has given.

My online home is https://www.pjfiala.com.
You can connect with me on Facebook at https://www.facebook.com/PJFiala1,
and
Instagram at https://www.Instagram.com/PJFiala.
If you prefer to email, go ahead, I'll respond - pjfiala@pjfiala.com.

83843957R00174